The Adventures of Gorrin the Gnome

A.M. Singleton

Bloomington, IN Milton Keynes, UK

authorHOUSE®

AuthorHouse™
1663 Liberty Drive, Suite 200
Bloomington, IN 47403
www.authorhouse.com
Phone: 1-800-839-8640

AuthorHouse™ UK Ltd.
500 Avebury Boulevard
Central Milton Keynes, MK9 2BE
www.authorhouse.co.uk
Phone: 08001974150

This book is a work of fiction. People, places, events, and situations are the product of the author's imagination. Any resemblance to actual persons, living or dead, or historical events, is purely coincidental.

First published by AuthorHouse 2/13/2006

ISBN: 1-4259-1370-9 (sc)

Printed in the United States of America
Bloomington, Indiana

This book is printed on acid-free paper.

To Natalie

Table of Contents

To all of Gorrin's friends who read the first drafts of the novel.

Chapter One
"The Awakening"

The monster moved over the earth and headed for the old copse of trees with its teeth pointing menacingly forwards. The ground trembled as the monster moved towards its intended victim - the trees. Of course the trees could do nothing but stand and stare helplessly at the yellow shape, smoke billowing from its single nostril into the cold still air.

Birds flew out of the trees to a safe distance and squirrels chattered frantically as the spluttering shape lurched towards them.

Finally, the monster reached the trees and as they splintered and cracked, they fell to the ground with a great welter of stones and earth. With a last defiant protest, the squirrels raced away from the scene over the surrounding grass and earth and headed for the next clump of trees.

Tom was the bulldozer driver, whose job it was to demolish this particular group of trees. He had been responsible for the wholesale demolition of a large number of such wooded areas in this part of the country. Working in pairs he was part of a number of demolition gangs clearing land ready for housing and road development.

He enjoyed his work as a bulldozer driver and he particularly liked the way the trees would come crashing down. The branches and leaves flailing through the air until they hit the ground with a great crash, as his monstrous machine moved ever onwards.

This particular copse was actually extremely old and was all that remained of a very ancient forest that used to cover this part of the country. Its original name was the Arden Forest, but now there was little of this large forest still remaining. So it was with some surprise that Gorrin the Gnome awoke from his slumber in a very sudden manner.

Gorrin had been sleeping quite peacefully for some time, though it wasn't sleep as you or I know it, but more of a hibernation. In short, he had been asleep for a little over three hundred and fifty years, and even for a gnome that was a very long time.

When he was last awake, Gorrin had just returned from a visit to his family, some ten leagues to the south. Gorrin came from a medium size family and had three brothers and one sister. Of course, when he finally reached his home having journeyed on foot, he had been very tired. Not wishing to be disturbed for a little while he had placed a magic charm on himself.

Unfortunately for Gorrin, he had made a slight mistake in the charm, with the result that he had gone into hibernation.

As he was dreaming of a far off time, suddenly earth from his house ceiling started to sprinkle down on to his face. At first he just twitched - but as the sprinkle became first a shower, then a torrent of stones, peat clay then flowers, grass and various other unmentionables, he sat up with a start, spluttering and really quite shocked.

This was not unsurprising one might say, particularly when it was his home that appeared to be undergoing some rather sudden and major redecoration! A thunderous noise accompanied this deluge that sounded like a fire-breathing dragon to poor Gorrin.

As he tried to gather his wits about him, Gorrin became aware that daylight was now filtering down from above. The sun's rays were now clearly visible through what had once been his beautiful mud and lath plaster ceiling.

There was also a sharp and nasty smell that was completely unlike anything he had ever smelt in his entire life. This pungent smell was really quite unpleasant and it increased in strength as it rolled in through the hole.

As the mud and stone, together with the very bad smell continued to pour into his poor little house, the hole in his ceiling grew larger and larger. Daylight was now flooding into the bedroom making it quite light inside and there was no need of a lamp to see the way.

Gorrin threw off his bedclothes and shot across the remains of his bedroom into an adjoining room. He gathered up his outdoor clothes and as he did this his red and white striped nightgown ruffled around him and his white nightcap fell off.

Quickly he left this room and headed down a corridor that sloped downwards until it reached what was Gorrin's parlour. When he got to the parlour, he rapidly dressed, but as he did so he realised he had forgotten his shiny black boots. He remembered that he had left the boots close to the front door of his house - or at least what remained of his house.

Quick as a flash, Gorrin ran as fast as his little legs could carry him. This was really quite fast as he was only seven hundred and five, and that is really quite young for a Gnome. His father had been nearly fifteen hundred when he last saw him and it was not uncommon for gnomes to live for at least two thousand years.

As he neared the entrance, it became more and more difficult as rock, soil and other debris lay in his path, but still he struggled onwards.

It was at this point he started to think that maybe it was not such a good idea after all to try to get his favourite black boots. Even so, he was not going to be bested by some nasty smelling dragon, so he carried on until he finally reached his old front door.

There sticking forlornly out of the earth were his boots - quickly he scooped them up and retraced his steps back through the tunnels.

Meanwhile, Tom was having a fine old time on the surface - trees were crashing down, earth was flying everywhere and to his mind, all was right with the world. As he continued on, he was suddenly aware of his mate Patrick, who was waving his arms frantically, trying to attract his attention.

At first, Tom thought he would ignore Patrick and pretend he had not seen him. Patrick decided that Tom was either deliberately not seeing him or he really hadn't seen him. Either way he had better try a different tack at trying to attract Tom's attention.

Patrick, ran around to the front of the bulldozer and continued to flail his arms about - this was really quite a stupid thing to do as anyone who knows will tell you

- bulldozers don't take prisoners, they just squash you flat.

Luckily for Patrick, Tom had actually seen him and decided that he had better stop and find out what it was all about. As he switched off the engine and the vibrating machine shuddered to a halt the silence that descended was almost deafening after such a horrible noise.

Tom paused, and then said, "Well, what is it that makes you want to be squashed by my pride and joy?"

Patrick, paused before answering ... "There has been a terrible mistake," he said. "This is the wrong clump of trees, it should be that one over there," he said pointing to another group of trees.

"What do you mean the wrong trees?" said Tom.

"Ummm, I think I had the plan upside down," replied Patrick. "We'll be for it now!" he said.

"Well this is a proper mess that you got us into isn't it. And how do you think we are going to talk our way out of this one? I'm damn sure the boss is not going to be pleased, one little bit" Tom replied.

"Ummm - I suppose he won't be," said Patrick."

"Well state the obvious" said Tom, "Look, unless we tell him, he isn't going to know.... at least not for a while anyway ... and by then one of the other work gangs might get the blame." Tom stood for a moment thinking before replying and then said, "Yes, that's what we'll do - we say nothing and hope no one spots it until we are well away working where we should be."

"OK" Patrick said, "If you are sure?"

"Just make sure that the next clump of trees we knock down are the right ones - or I'll give you a thick ear, make no mistake," Tom finished.

With that, the two got back on the bulldozer and started to head for the next clump of trees that lay about a quarter of a mile away. The machine continued pumping smelly fumes into the clear sky and clanking as it headed away from Gorrin's demolished home.

As the bulldozer receded from the copse, Gorrin stuck his head up above the ground. He was now dressed in a smart red tunic with trousers to match and his shiny black boots. He spotted the two who had woken him up so rudely, and then proceeded to turn his once lovely little home underground, into a complete shambles.

"Rats!" exclaimed Gorrin, "So those are the buffoons who disturbed me! Well I'll give them something to think about." Quickly, he returned to his home and headed for his storeroom that was next to his kitchen, climbing across the debris that now littered his tunnels and rooms.

He opened the cupboard door and took off the shelves a number of things that were carefully stored there. From the many items stored there, he selected a purple velvet pouch, then a shiny white gold ring, with a finely set amethyst.

As he continued to look at the different items stored there, he also picked up, a small leather satchel, and finally a shaped walking stick made of blackthorn. Blackthorn is a very hard wood that is better known as the sloe tree, and that is where the sloe berries that go into making sloe wine come from.

He picked up the stick, he looked at the runes carved into the surface and smiled a secret sort of smile. The runes inscribed into the surface of the stick were an ancient language several thousands of years old. This was the language that many of the magic charms and incantations were written in.

He then turned on his heel and headed back to the surface, this time using the concealed back door that lay at the base of an old knarled oak tree.

He looked over at the receding figures of the two who had caused him so much trouble and took a pinch of strangely glittering powder out of the purple velvet pouch. He threw the powder up into the air so that it landed upon him; while at the same time he muttered a short incantation.

With an odd pop! Gorrin sparkled and disappeared, and almost as suddenly, he reappeared in the copse of trees towards which the two unsuspecting workers were headed.

Carefully concealing himself, Gorrin carefully observed and waited for the bulldozer to approach. Gorrin had realised from watching the two men that the bulldozer was not a dragon, but was some sort of machine - and a dirty smelly one it was too.

As the bulldozer approached, the trees, the machine slowed to a halt and stopped. The driver of the bulldozer then switched off the engine so that he could talk to the other man. As the engine stopped it became very quiet. The breeze through the branches of the trees in the copse was all that could now be heard.

As Gorrin listened, he understood two things. First, they were both strangely dressed, and second, they were speaking strangely. Although as he listened it became obvious to him that one of them was speaking with an accent that was reminiscent of one of his old friends.

As he listened, his mind flew back across the years and he remembered his old friend Seamus, from across the water.

Seamus was an old childhood friend who just happened to be a leprechaun. As Gorrin's thoughts continued to wander, he realised he had not seen him for a good many years. Exactly how long he had not seen him, he was not sure, since he did not know how long he had been asleep.

Gorrin was bought back to the present, with the realisation that the two men talking were discussing that they intended to demolish the trees he was currently hiding within. As Gorrin listened, he also realised that they had demolished his home accidentally and that they were still arguing over whose fault it was.

As he digested this information, he became angrier that these two idiots had managed to wreck his home and the ancient woodland in which it was hidden. He was especially annoyed that they had also smashed the trees down and made the birds, squirrels and other animals homeless.

"Right" he said to no one in particular, "now to teach those two buffoons a lesson, they won't forget in a hurry." He took his ring out of his tunic pocket and slipped it on to his finger, as he did so he muttered an ancient charm and rubbed the amethyst. One second, he was kneeling behind the tree, and then he began to shimmer and fade away until nothing could be seen.

Gorrin stood up, and carefully walked over to where the two men were standing. As he did so, he picked up a few small stones and these disappeared from view as he touched them.

Carefully taking aim, he threw the first small stone at Tom. As the stone flew through the air, it reappeared and to all intents and purposes had just magically appeared out of thin air as it hit Tom plumb on the nose.

Whack! "Ouch!" exclaimed Tom, "What did you do that for?"

"What do mean, do what?" said Patrick.

"Throw that stone," replied Tom.

"I never did!" said Patrick.

Just then another small missile appeared out of thin air, this time it hit Patrick on the top of his head.

"Hey, that hurt," said Patrick. "Now who's throwing stones?"

The words had barely left his mouth, when a small stick appeared and landed between the pair, at which point they both looked round and stared at the copse. They both turned to look at each other and a wicked glint appeared in both their eyes, then they started to walk towards the trees.

"Come out come out wherever you are!" shouted Tom, "We know your little game!"

Just then another stone appeared just before it hit Tom smartly on the back of his hand. "Ow!" Tom said. "Right if that's the way you want to play it!"   Tom immediately headed for the trees.

There was, of course, nobody there, so he ran to the next tree and the next, and so on looking for the mysterious assailant.

Meanwhile, Gorrin had continued to bombard Patrick with whatever he could lay his hands on, small stones, acorns, and even dried animal dung. This made the best missile of all as it had a tendency to explode in a rather unpleasant cloud of dust. One managed to find its mark right on top of Patrick's head, momentarily stunning him both with the accuracy and of course the smell!

As this was happening just outside the copse, Tom had been unsuccessful in trying to find the unknown attacker, so he returned to the edge of the wood. Even as Tom had returned, Gorrin had himself doubled back into the copse. As he entered the copse, he had spotted a wasp nest up in the trees, with just a few remaining wasps buzzing around the entrance to the nest.

Gorrin pointed his walking stick towards the nest and uttered a phrase; where-upon a jet of green light flew from the end to sever neatly the anchorage of the nest. "Sorry fellows," said Gorrin, "But my need is greater." The nest having been parted from the tree, headed earthwards to burst close to where Tom was standing.

Immediately the wasps exited from the shattered remains of their nest. As they did so, they saw two figures close by - Tom and Patrick - and as quick as anything they started to attack the two, as they thought had attacked and destroyed their nest.

Quickly, the pair started to try to beat off the wasps and to run towards the bulldozer. By the time they actually reached it they were both well and truly stung, but still the wasps continued to dive bomb them.

Tom scrambled in one side of the bulldozer cab and Patrick the other side, both slamming the doors. The engine roared into life and the yellow monster, started to move away as fast as it could go, clanking and belching smoke as it went.

As it retreated into the distance, Gorrin had a half smile on his face, "That's one lesson they will not forget in a hurry," he said. With that he turned and trudged back towards his own particular copse of trees and for a well-earned breakfast of freshly picked woodland fruits and mushrooms, his favourite food.

~~~~~~~~~~~

Chapter Two
"Breakfast & Departure"

Gorrin reached his own woodland home, to find his front door well and truly blocked by fallen trees and soil. Carefully picking his way through the tangle of branches he went around to his back door and entered.

Once inside he went straight to his kitchen and started to look for his trug. This was a small basket that he used for picking mushrooms and fruit. There was little daylight filtering through the small window, as the pane was very dirty. It was coated in years of grime and this limited the amount of light and what he could actually see. Looking around for a suitable cloth, he found an old rag, but this was completely useless, as it had almost rotted away.

He went back outside and picked a couple of large maple leaves from a tree. Then he set to work to use the leaves to wipe away the years of grime on the small pane of glass. The windowpane was set into a bank of earth that was covered in wild mushrooms.

As a very knowledgeable gnome, he knew which mushrooms were poisonous and which were edible. Carefully avoiding damaging the mushrooms, Gorrin cleaned the small pane of glass.

When he had finished cleaning the glass, he returned to his kitchen. "Good" Gorrin said to himself. "Now I can see a little better." Then, he started to look around for the trug. The trug was a basket woven out of willow and had been given to him by his sister a long time ago. Gorrin normally used the little trug to collect his picked woodland fruit and mushrooms.

Gorrin could not remember where he had last put his trug, as it had been a very long time since he had last used it. Of course, Gorrin did not know how long, but he suspected that it was quite a long time.

After a lot of searching around his kitchen, he eventually discovered the trug hiding at the back of a small pantry on the floor. Just as he reached in to pick it up, there was a loud crash! He dodged backwards, just missing the shelf that had just come crashing down to the floor. Unfortunately for Gorrin, he wasn't quite quick enough, and a small cauldron landed upside down on his head, just like a hat.

With that he fell over backwards, his legs frantically flailing about and landed in a heap on the floor. He sat there on the floor wearing the cauldron as a hat for a few seconds. His poor head was spinning as it had hit him with quite a blow.

When his head had finally stopped spinning, he tried to remove the cauldron. "Oh no," he thought, "It won't come off." He stood up, but try as he might, as he wrestled with the cauldron trying to remove it from his head, it would not budge.

Gorrin's ears were pinned inside it and were preventing him from removing the cauldron from his head. Every time he tried, it pulled on his ears and that hurt, as his ears were very sensitive.

After trying really hard for about five minutes to remove the cauldron, he sat on one of his kitchen stools and rested. He was now in a real grump and for Gorrin that was quite unusual. "What was he to do?" he thought. Then he had an idea "What about soap? Yes of course," he said to himself, "Why didn't I think of that before?"

He stood up and walked over to the kitchen sink, but didn't see that on the floor was a bar of old soap. He stood on it, and before he could stop himself, his leg shot from under him. Down went Gorrin and he hit the floor. Bang! The cauldron hit the floor and his head rang like a bell. The cauldron cracked and then broke into two pieces while poor Gorrin laid upon the floor. His head was now pounding like a steam hammer from the loud bell like noise the cauldron had made.

Groggily, Gorrin carefully stood up and he rubbed his ears, which were very sore from all the pulling. His aching head gradually got better and he stepped gingerly over to the pantry, looking at the other shelves. He did not want to risk anything else landing on his head, so he very slowly picked up the basket. Just as he did so, there was another creak.

He moved more quickly this time and this was just as well, as the other two shelves decided that they had had enough as well as the first shelf. They were going to try to hit Gorrin on the head also. Fortunately for Gorrin, they missed, however, more pots, pans and clay jars headed for the floor.

Once the noise of all the shelves falling down had subsided, Gorrin stood and looked at the scene. "What a mess!" he thought to himself. "That is going to take quite some cleaning to sort that lot out."

Gorrin headed back outside, this time with his small trug and he started to gather the wild cooking mushrooms he had spotted earlier. Of course, he collected only the edible fungi and not the poisonous varieties.

Once he had collected enough woodland mushrooms, he moved further out into the wood looking for berries. He managed to find some wild plums and small crab apples, as well as a few alpine strawberries. As he picked the strawberries, he thought to himself that it was very unusual to find strawberries this late in the year.

With his little basket filled with the interesting assortment of fruit and fungi, he started back to his home. He was aware of the sound of birds calling to one another and the squirrels, scampering along the branches of the trees had returned to his home.

When he entered his kitchen, he took out his tinderbox and opened it. Inside the tinderbox there was his flint, steel and dried bark shavings mixed with plant fibres. He took a small quantity of the fibre mixture and using his flint and steel drew the flint smartly across the steel.

Fine sparks showered on to the kindling and he blew carefully into the bundle. The sparks glowed then burst into flame. Quickly he placed the burning wad into the fireplace and covered it with small twigs. Very soon he had a good fire burning in his fireplace and he added more branches on to the fire.

While the fire was now burning well, Gorrin started to prepare the fruit for his breakfast. First he went to the sink and started to pump the handle of the water siphon pump, but he quickly realised that the leather washers inside the pump were dry so it would not work. The pump had not been used for a very long time, so the washers inside had dried out. This was not a problem though, as in one of the many deep underground rooms there was a spring. He picked up an old wooden pail and took a candle from a shelf in the kitchen. He lit the candle from the fireplace and walked along the short corridor that led into the larder room.

In the larder room was a small spring that welled up out of the ground and across a stone channel to run down into a hole at the far end, from where it reappeared in the wood as a small stream. He placed his wooden pail under the stream of water and filled his bucket.

Once back in his kitchen he poured some of the water into the sink and washed his hands with the soap and water. Having dried them on a small moss towel, Gorrin then washed the fruit and mushrooms and started to carefully slice the apples into small pieces.

The plums were then de-stoned, the strawberries hulled and the fruit then placed into a bowl. He enjoyed hulling strawberries - this was the process of removing the green leaves and shoots. The best part was when he had finished hulling and he could lick the juice off his fingers

The mushrooms were sliced and then placed into a frying pan and the fruit added to the pan. Gorrin picked up the frying pan and placed it on to the griddle over the fire to cook. Very soon the sweet smell of fruit mixed with mushrooms floated into the air from the frying pan as the mixture heated.

After the fruit and mushrooms had been cooking for about ten minutes, Gorrin carefully picked up the pan and poured the contents into a bowl he had previously placed on to his kitchen table.

Gorrin poured himself a cup of water from the wooden pail, had a long drink from it and then placed it on to the table. With that he sat down at the kitchen table and proceeded to eat his breakfast. As he started eating, he began to think about the events of the morning.

It was obvious to him, that the world had changed greatly since he had gone to sleep. The language the men had spoken was strangely different, as was their clothing, to say nothing of the strange yellow machine that the two men had been riding. This strange machine was evidence that much had altered.

As he finished his meal, he sat back and thought about his family, wondering where they were and what they might be doing. He still had no real idea as to how long he had been asleep for, but first things first.

He stood up and washed the bowl and spoon and put them away, then started to clear up the mess in his kitchen. Clearing up all of the mess took him the rest of the morning and by the time he had finished it was nearly noon.

He peered out of the kitchen window at the sky and noticed something strange moving across it. The object seemed to be very high up in the air and left a cloudy trail behind it, but Gorrin had no idea what was making those strange lines in the sky.

Gorrin went over to where he had left his special walking stick and tapped the end smartly on the floor three times and muttered in the strange ancient language. The end of the stick immediately began to glow, faintly at first then brighter and brighter. Eventually, it was so bright it lit up the entire kitchen with a blue white light.

With the stick firmly held aloft, Gorrin went back to the room where the special magical objects were kept and picked up another velvet pouch. The pouch he picked up was green in colour and contained a green sparkling powder.

He took the pouch and walked carefully along the corridor to his bedroom. He looked up at the ceiling and stared at the large gaping hole in his ceiling which was plainly visible. He took a pinch of the powder out of the green pouch and sang softly as he threw the powder into the air.

The powder flew through the air, glittering as it did so. Nothing appeared to happen at first, and then one piece of soil and mud on the floor rose up into the air and stuck to the edge of the hole. This was followed quickly, with another, then another at an ever-increasing rate, until the hole was filled completely and it looked almost as good as new.

Gorrin looked about the bedroom and saw the dishevelled bed and since he was a tidy gnome thought that he should make his bed. He walked over to the painting of his family that was lying upon the floor. Picking it up carefully, he replaced it back on to the wall from where it had fallen when the ceiling had started falling in.

A little more tidying up was required, but finally he was finished. Gorrin then returned to his kitchen and put out the light coming from the walking stick, by rapping it three times upon the floor.

Gorrin sat down at the kitchen table staring into the glowing embers of the fire wondered how long he had been asleep. The first thing he needed to do was contact his family and so he got up and went to a small shelf and retrieved a number of smoky coloured highly polished stones and he placed all, but one, on to the kitchen table. He then sat back down at the table.

Holding the remaining stone in the palm of his hand he spoke to the communicator sunstone the names of his family. The stone seemed to glow on its surface for a brief moment, but then the stone went dark. He frowned at this and thought for a few more moments about what he was going to do. He hadn't a clue, but he needed to find out before he went looking for his family.

As he continued to stare into the fire, Gorrin's mind wandered back to the past. He remembered those sunny summer days when he had sat out in the late afternoon sunshine sipping sloe wine with his old friends.

His mind quickly returned to the present as the embers collapsed in a flurry of sparks that floated up the chimney. He decided that he needed to visit the nearest town, wherever that now was, since he was sure that things had changed quite a lot since he was last walking across the country.

Gorrin stood up from the chair he had been sitting on, with a clear idea of what he was going to do. The nearest main town to his home was Stratford-upon-Avon - or at least it used to be. That was where he decided to go to see what had become of the world during his years of slumber.

Picking up a beeswax candle from the shelf that was beside the kitchen table, he placed it carefully into the candleholder. Next he took a wax dip and lit it in the fireplace and proceeded to light the main beeswax candle.

When it had caught alight, he blew out the wax dip and replaced it on to the shelf. Picking up the candleholder he carefully walked along to his store cupboard to gather a few supplies for his intended journey.

First he needed a backpack to carry the more bulky items, as well as food for the journey. There were still a few jars of dried fruits, which were sealed and carefully preserved with a magic charm to stop the fruit from going bad.

He picked up the jars and placed them into his backpack. As he rummaged though the cupboard and little drawers within it, he picked out an assortment of little tools that were likely to come in handy.

Glinting at the back of the cupboard he spotted a jar of liniment. This was a paste that was used to mend cuts and bruises quickly. This was no ordinary paste however, as it had magical properties and could soothe and mend the skin in only a couple of minutes.

Having packed a few more items that he thought might be useful, a sudden thought occurred to him. He had better get something to write with as well. This was because Gorrin had always kept a journal of all his travels, and since this was likely to be quite an adventure, then he was going to make sure that he kept a record of it.

Gorrin left the kitchen picking up the candleholder with the beeswax candle still burning brightly in it and headed for the parlour where his writing desk was.

There in the corner of the parlour was the mahogany-veneered writing desk. Carefully opening the cover, he lowered it down. As he did this, two small wooden supports came out of the front to support the writing surface.

Peering inside he looked at the green leather surface, then at the small compartments at the back. He opened the left hand one and there inside was his small penknife. This was normally used to sharpen his quill pen. Lying next to the penknife was a quill and small bottle of ink. Those might be useful, he thought, but he needed some scrolls of parchment paper to go with them.

Looking around in one of the other drawers he found three rolls of parchment that were tied up with red ribbon. He placed the ink; quill, penknife and parchment into a small carry case that he had found in the very bottom drawer of the writing bureau. Picking the carry case up, Gorrin returned to the kitchen and packed the small carry case into the backpack.

Anyone looking at the scene would have noticed something very strange about the number of items that Gorrin had placed into the backpack. Not matter how many things he put into the pack; it did not seem to get full. This was not surprising as the backpack was enchanted and could store many things much larger than the apparent amount of space contained within the pack.

The backpack had been a present from the Queen of the Faerie and her people, for a help against a powerful dark magician. He had been presented with the backpack as a thank you, to help him when he travelled far from home. The backpack was likely to be very useful in his travels.

There was one final thing that Gorrin needed before he set off on his journey - something to drink of course. He walked over to the draining board that was set next to the stone sink in the kitchen and picked up an old ale skin. This was specially waterproofed to hold any liquid, whether it was ale or water. As Gorrin had no ale, he would have to settle for water.

Gorrin went back to the spring room where the water was cascading merrily down on to the stone trough and filled his ale skin with the cool crystal clear water. Once filled, he corked the ale skin and slung it over his shoulder using the leather strap attached to it, and returned to the kitchen. He picked up his backpack and walked towards his back door. Taking a last wistful look around his home Gorrin opened the back door and stepped outside.

He closed the door and using his walking stick pointed at the door with the one end and sang softly. As he sang, the runes on the walking stick glowed blue and a blue beam of light sprang from the tip of the stick. As the beam of light struck the door, the protection charm took hold and the doorway faded from sight until no trace of it was visible. The door was still there, but hidden from view and protected by the enchantment.

Gorrin stood looking at where his home lay hidden from view, then turned on his heel and started to walk in the direction of the nearest town over the fields. He started to walk, but then paused briefly to look up into the sky and he caught sight of another one of those strange cloud lines high up in the sky. He still didn't know what these strange clouds were or what they meant, but that was just one more puzzle to ponder. With that he started to walk again towards new places and adventures.

~~~~~~~~~~~~~~~~~

Chapter Three
"The Canal and the Cyclist"

Gorrin walked over the ploughed fields in a roughly southerly direction and looked all around him, wondering at the huge size of the fields. Last time he had been out walking the fields had been much smaller and there had been more hedgerows to hide in. He was feeling a little exposed as he continued walking across one very large field. After several hours of walking Gorrin noticed that he was approaching a line of trees that seemed to run north to south.

This unusual straight line of trees looked interesting he thought, and as he got closer to the line of trees, he noticed something odd. There were two sets of trees that were parallel to each other running along in a straight line. He was used to seeing meandering rivers with trees either side, but not in such a straight line.

Once he reached the tree line it became obvious to him that there was indeed water between the two sets of trees but that this particular river was exceptionally straight. He also realised that one side of this river had a path and the other side did not. The other strange thing was that the water did not appear to be flowing in any direction and this fact did not seem to bother the mallard ducks that were swimming merrily along, quacking as they went.

Gorrin climbed down to the path beside the water through a gap in the trees and bushes and then stood next to the water. "Well," he thought, "Here was a ready made footpath" and so started to walk along it in a southerly direction again. He walked at quite a brisk jaunty pace and started to whistle merrily. After about a mile and a half he reached a brick built bridge that crossed over the water. Just as he was walking through under it, he heard a strange noise of something moving over the gravel path.

Damien was an arrogant boy of fifteen who was very tall for his age and he really liked to cycle, particularly along the canal towpath. As well as being arrogant, he had a vindictive sense of humour, and so when he saw a small figure in a red tunic, red jacket and black boots, he thought he would have some fun by trying to cause him to fall into the water. He deliberately speeded up and as he neared the boy in red, aimed for him so that he could knock him into the water. The figure in red did not see the approaching Damien until it was too late.

The strange noise approached Gorrin at quite a speed and before he realised it, the noise was upon him. Bearing down on him was a person dressed in shiny clothing with a strange helmet on and this person was riding some sort of two-wheeled machine. Before he was able to get out of the way properly, Gorrin was knocked off his feet and was now sailing through the air towards the water.

It all seemed to happen in slow motion and he could not stop himself, when splash! Gorrin was in the water coughing and spluttering as he surfaced. Luckily gnomes are very buoyant and he floated quite well, though much to Gorrin's disgust and annoyance, the cyclist was continuing along the towpath away from him laughing.

Gorrin grabbed hold of the grass and reeds and clambered out of the water on to the bank, water dripping from his clothing. The water was very cold and tasted very unpleasant as it had an oily sheen floating on its surface. In the sunlight, he was aware of the rainbow of colours dancing on the surface, of the water but this did not really compensate him for the nasty taste he now had in his mouth. Something was moving in one of his large pockets and he put his hand inside and pulled out a fish. Before he could stop it, the fish had jumped back into the water and swam away.

Cold and dripping wet he glared reproachfully at the retreating figure of the cyclist and turned his back to continue walking along the towpath. That was one 'favour' he was definitely going to repay to the cyclist at the earliest opportunity. In the meantime he continued to walk along the towpath. Gorrin was suddenly conscious of a chugging noise that was in the distance at the moment, but slowly approaching him. He decided that he should use his magic ring to become invisible until the strange noise had passed him by. He quickly chanted the ancient charm and then rubbed the amethyst on the ring.

After a few minutes he could see some sort of boat moving along the canal towards him, and as he continued to look as he walked, he realised that there was a figure standing at the rear of the boat that appeared to be steering it. The boat drew closer and it became obvious that this vessel was long and thin, and was brightly painted with flowers in pots on the roof of the boat.

Gorrin stood still and watched transfixed as the canal boat chugged past - he was fascinated by the way the craft moved through the water without a horse to pull it or sails to move it. As it passed, the nasty smell that he had smelt before from the strange yellow machine that had woken him up made its presence known to him and his nose wrinkled as he pulled a face. He really did not like this smell at all - this was probably that it was now associated with the bad memory of his rude awakening.

He had started to shiver from the cold and wet clothing he wore - Gorrin needed to either get dry or change his clothing, and it did not matter which, as long as he did it fairly soon, otherwise he might catch a cold. Gorrin decided to leave the track and get to the other side of the trees and bushes that lined the canal. As he struggled through the brambles and over the small fence, he found himself in another field, though this was not as large as the one he had recently left.

Looking around for kindling, Gorrin gathered together a small pile of twigs and smaller branches and then he built a small pyramid. Pointing his walking stick at the pile he sang a little song - this time the runes on the staff glowed red and a red flame shot out of the end to ignite the dry pile of kindling. Normally, he would have used the tinderbox rather than magic to make a fire, but the tinderbox had leaked, as the lid had not been secured properly.

As he warmed himself on the fire he realised that it must be late in the day, the sun was sinking over the horizon, an orange-red ball in the sky. He removed his very wet jacket and placed it on to a stick he had previously stuck into the ground making sure that whilst the jacket was able to dry, it would not get so close to the fire to burn.

He pulled a blanket out of his backpack and then pulled off his boots and tipped the remaining water out on to the grass. His little trousers needed to be dried also, so quickly he took them off and hung them in front of the fire to dry also. While the red clothes were drying in front of the fire, he went back to his backpack and took out a towel and dried himself before taking out a green coloured jacket and trousers. Once dry, he put on the jacket and trousers and as he gradually warmed up, his teeth stopped chattering from the cold, so he was then able to comb his beard, after first drying it.

Now warmer and dry, he took out a jar with dried fruit in it and started munching on dried plums and dried apricots and a few biscuits, followed by a drink of water out of the ale skin. He looked up at the lengthening shadows as the sun gradually set. He wrapped the blanket around himself and settled down on the grass and took out a roll of parchment and started to write down what had happened to him today. Topping up the fire with more sticks, Gorrin continued to write with his ink and quill.

By the time that Gorrin had completed writing up the day's adventures, dusk had fallen and night was fast approaching. As the darkness grew, Gorrin was aware that the air was now quite cool and smelt like late September. He huddled closer to the fire and gradually nodded off to sleep.

In the early hours of the morning he awoke with a start and looked around. The mist eddied around his little campsite and the fire was almost out. Gorrin could hear a strange rustling noise coming out of the mist. The mist made it difficult to see the source of the strange noise.

Gorrin continued to stare into the mist and stood up, picking up his wooden staff as he did so. He held on tight to the staff and slowly walked into the mist towards the sound. He could feel his heartbeat pounding away in his chest as he nervously moved towards the sound.

Gradually a large shape became visible, then another and another. He began to get a little concerned and pointed the staff at the shapes. He made ready to start singing a charm, when he was suddenly aware that three pairs of large brown eyes were staring at him through the mist. The shape that was closest to him without warning made a loud moo!

It was with a great relief that he lowered his wooden staff and started to smile, and then he laughed a huge laugh of relief. Imagine being scared by a herd of cows, now whatever next he thought. I will get frightened of my own shadow at this rate. He lowered his staff and went back to what was left of his fire. Looking about in the gloomy mist, he picked up a few more branches and placed them on to the embers and carefully blew until the twigs burst into flame. He continued to pile a few more branches on to the flames and then sat down gathering his blanket up and wrapping it around himself like a shawl.

Gorrin started to think about what he was going to do the next day as he did gazed into the fire. While he continued to stare at the dancing flames, his eyes got heavier and heavier and he started to nod off back to sleep. Within a few minutes he was fast asleep. The cows that had been curious as to who was in their field, looked on for a short while before they grew bored and wandered off back into the mist.

Dawn came gradually through the swirling mist and the sound of the birds singing the dawn chorus, though the mist muted it, roused Gorrin from his sleep. He opened his eyes but he couldn't remember where he was for a few seconds. It all came back to him in a rush and he sat up as he remembered the past night's events. He then stood up and looked at the fire, the embers of which were just glowing. Searching around the campsite area, he gathered together more twigs and placed them on to the fire and carefully blew on the embers. The twigs set alight and started to crackle and smoke as they burned.

Now that his little fire was again burning nicely, he set about looking for some field mushrooms for his breakfast. As he wandered around the field looking for the fungi, he was aware that the mist was slowly lifting, as the sun was gradually rising into the sky. He could not see the sun clearly because of the mist, but could make out where it was by the way the mist glowed. Gorrin managed to find quite a nice collection of field mushrooms and he carefully picked them and placed them into one of his pockets, as he had forgotten to pack his trug.

The mist continued to lift while he walked back to his little campsite and he became aware of shapes in the far end of the field. For a couple of seconds he wondered what these shapes were and his eyebrows furrowed as he frowned. As he remembered the events of the previous night he smiled, "It was the cows of course," he thought.

Back at his campsite, he opened the backpack and took out his little cooking pan and opened one of the jars of preserved fruit he carried. Putting the fruit into the cooking pan he placed it into the fire carefully. He took the field mushrooms out of his pocket and using a small knife cut up the fungi into small pieces and placed these into the cooking pan with the fruit that was already beginning to steam.

Looking again in his backpack, he found a wooden spoon and started to stir the mixture in the pan, mashing up the fruit as he did so, the juices mixing with the mushrooms as it started to boil. Gorrin let the mixture boil for a few minutes, to make sure that the mushrooms were properly cooked.

While his breakfast was cooking, he took a drink of water out of his ale skin. Feeling refreshed from the cold liquid, he looked at his breakfast cooking. After waiting a few more moments, he took the pan off the fire and placed it on to the grass. This caused the dew on the grass to hiss as the hot pan heated it. Looking again in his backpack, Gorrin pulled out a wooden bowl and then poured the hot mixture in the cooking pan into the bowl.

Sitting back down on his small leather mat in a cross-legged fashion, Gorrin started to eat his breakfast while listening to the sounds around him. The mist by this time was fading fast, but was still sufficiently thick to prevent him from seeing the bottom of the field where the cows were, although he could hear them moving around. He became aware as he sat eating, of a chugging sound coming from the direction of the canal and it was coming closer and closer.

He quickly finished his breakfast and packed up all of his camp things into his backpack, then looked at his campsite. Hmm, he thought, he had better put things back as they were before he camped. Picking up some of the earth around the fire he covered the embers with the soil to smother it. Rummaging in his backpack he pulled out an old wooden cup and walked towards the pond that was in the field.

The cows were now drinking from the pond and they gazed across at him as he scooped water up into the cup and then walked back to his fire. He poured the water over the fire, the remaining embers protested by hissing back at him. Now the fire was out and he needed to repair the burnt grass.

Gorrin put his hand into one of his pockets and took out the small green velvet pouch. This pouch contained the faerie powder he had used to repair his bedroom. Carefully opening the drawstring of the bag, he took out a pinch of the green sparkling powder and sprinkled it over the fire, singing softly as he did so. The air glittered as the powder covered the now wet and cold fire.

As before, nothing appeared to happen at first, but then the edges of the burned soil began to sprout blades of grass. Within a minute, the entire area where the fire had been was now back as it had been before the fire. He replaced the velvet pouch back into his jacket pocket.

Gorrin looked at his handiwork "Good," he said out loud. "Not a bad job if I say so myself"."

Picking up his backpack, he put the red clothes he had been wearing yesterday, when he had been knocked into the canal, into the backpack. They were almost dry, but he hadn't time to wait for them to finish drying, as he wanted to be on his way. With his backpack now firmly strapped to his back, he said goodbye to the cows who had now returned to his campsite. They gazed at him with their large brown eyes and went "Moo!" as if to say goodbye.

Climbing carefully over the small fence and through the bushes and trees that lined the canal-side, Gorrin stepped down on to the towpath and started to walk south again. This time he kept a wary eye open for any two-wheeled machines, either behind him or in front of him. There were still traces of mist hanging over the water, and in some places the mist was still a quite thick, like floating cotton wool.

After he had been walking for about half an hour he heard the sound of another boat moving towards him. Just as he walked under another bridge, he spotted the vessel moving along at a steady pace, but it was still several hundred yards away.

The boat was painted green and had a large yellow name 'Green Finch' neatly painted on the sides. There was a man steering the boat who was dressed in a thick red and green woollen sweater and as the boat drew nearer, the boatman noticed the small figure walking along the towpath. As the boat reached the green figure the boatman's attention was taken by the strange green clothing that the figure was wearing.

At first he thought that it was a child wearing fancy dress, but then he realised that it was a small man as the 'child' had a silvery grey beard! The boatman turned around to stare at the figure in green on the towpath, as his boat chugged past.

Meanwhile, Gorrin had been watching the approach of the canal boat as he continued to walk along the towpath. When the boat drew level with him, he noticed that the boatman was staring at him in a strange fashion. Gorrin stopped walking and looked back at the boat as it receded from him. He smiled at the boatman and the boatman then smiled back.

Gorrin started to walk again and the boatman continued to stare at the little figure until he realised he was about to hit the bank and had to make a sudden course correction. By the time he had managed to prevent running aground, the figure had vanished into the bright mist.

As the sun climbed into the sky, the mist continued to evaporate and the air grew warmer. A heron that had been standing on the towpath, looked at the small green figure that was walking along towards her. For a while the heron pretended that she had not noticed, but as the figure continued to walk towards her, she decided that she would fly away to a quieter spot.

With a great flapping of wings the large grey bird took off and circled before flying further along the canal away from the walking gnome. It landed about a hundred yards further along the towpath and looked back at the little figure.

Meanwhile along the same canal towpath, a cyclist was cycling along at a fairly brisk pace - it was Damien. He cycled along and spotted the heron and quickly decided to see how close he could get to the Heron before it flew off. Damien accelerated quickly and headed towards the heron.

The heron had been watching Gorrin and had not noticed the cyclist until it was within ten metres of her. She suddenly launched herself into the air, making a loud protest at the same time and it flew off over the trees and into the fields beyond. Damien thought that this was a really cool game and started to laugh, when he saw a small figure about a hundred metres further along the towpath in front of him.

Gorrin had seen the appearance of the cyclist and recognised the shiny clothing and hat of the person riding the two-wheeled machine. His eyes narrowed and he started to think fast. "What was he going to do?" he thought. It was obvious by the way the boy on the machine had just ridden at the heron, that this person was up to no good and would probably try to knock him into the water again. Then an idea occurred to him that he hoped would teach the cyclist a lesson. With the idea now firmly in his mind he smiled and continued to walk onwards towards the oncoming machine.

Damien was now pedalling furiously towards the small walking figure as he had every intention of knocking him into the water, just as he had done the previous late afternoon.

He got closer and closer until he reached him and swerved towards the green suited little man with the silver beard.

Just as Damien reached Gorrin and swerved towards him, Gorrin uttered a short verse and threw the strangely glittering powder that had had previously taken out of the purple velvet pouch into the air. 'Pop' he promptly disappeared from where he was standing and then reappeared about ten metres behind the cyclist.

Damien could not stop as he aimed his cycle at the little man, and was surprised when the figure went 'Pop!' and disappeared right in front of him. This so startled him he lost control of his cycle and the front wheel caught in the steel bank reinforcement and he was catapulted into the air.

As he sailed through the air, Damien started to regret what he had just tried to do, but of course it was now too late. He hit the water with a great 'Splash!' His cycle followed him and just missed his head before it sank out of sight. As he surfaced, coughing and spluttering he saw the bubbles rising from where his new bike was now resting - at the bottom of the canal!

Gorrin stood and watched to make sure that the cycle rider was not about to drown, but he quickly realised that the cyclist could swim, so he relaxed. Damien swam to the bank and climbed out of the freezing water. His cycle hat was decorated with mud and his mouth was full of a horrible taste.

He stood up, covered head to foot in mud and slime and started to shiver. Damien now looked across to where the bubbles were continuing to rise to the surface of the water and from where his cycle now lay. Just what was he going to tell him parents about his new bike?

Gorrin looked on and smiled at the now dejected figure of Damien, and said out loud, "Well wastrel, perhaps that will teach you consideration for others," adding "maybe" as an afterthought. With that he turned round and continued to walk in the direction that he was originally walking, leaving Damien dripping wet and feeling very sorry for himself and wondering what exactly a wastrel was!

~~~~~~~~~~~~~~~~~~~~~~~

Chapter Four
"Tomatoes and Canal Boats"

Walking along the road were two boys and a girl who were fond of causing as much trouble as possible. Today was an extra holiday because the school they normally attended was closed for teacher training. The three were now heading for the canal with a large bag full of rotten tomatoes and a box of stink bombs that they had bought from a local toyshop. They loved playing practical jokes on anyone they could and today was no exception.

They had the whole day off from school and they intended to have a lot of fun at the expense of anyone they could. James was speaking to his two other friends Simon and Sarah.

"Do you know where we are going?" James asked.

"The canal," said Sarah and Simon together, laughing.

"And what are we going to do there?" said James.

"Drop this lot on the boats as they go past the bridge," said Simon.

Sarah giggled then said "But won't we get into trouble?"

"Only if we get caught and I don't intend for that to happen," said James. "Anyway, "he continued, "We can always leg it down the lane and over the fields, they'll never catch us anyway."

The three continued to walk on along the country lane in silence, and then Simon said, "How many tomatoes do we have James?"

"Loads" replied James, "We'll be able to give them a real pasting, in fact they are really soft, and so they'll make a nice sticky mess."

"Good" said Sarah, and then added, "This will be our best one yet."

Soon they reached the bridge and looked down at the canal below, and there in the distance was a narrowboat chugging along towards them. As soon as they saw the narrowboat, they opened the bag of tomatoes and made ready with the stink bombs.

The boat slowly made it way towards the bridge, the lady at the tiller completely unaware of what lay in store for her and her boat. As she neared the bridge she sounded the horn and took a drink from her mug of tea, which was very welcome since she was quite thirsty.

She was quite proud of her narrowboat and was frequently seen cleaning and polishing it, as well as planting and watering the plants that grew in pots that were on the steel roof of the boat.

Suddenly, just as the front of the boat started to pass under the bridge three heads popped up over the side of the bridge parapet. Almost as suddenly, a deluge of soggy tomatoes rained down, spattering the boat and making a complete mess of all her nice clean boat. She was too astonished at first to do or say anything. It was not until she saw a little container hit the steel roof of the boat and shatter into very small pieces that she actually shouted in anger up at the heads that were now laughing.

The commotion that had been caused by the raining tomatoes had prompted her partner to come up to the steering compartment, just as the horrible smell of bad eggs from the stink bomb rolled along the deck and into where they were both standing. The smell was really bad and both pulled faces like they were sucking on a lemon, as the smell seemed to cling to them.

By the time the boat had managed to stop and the man had jumped off to give chase, the three on the bridge had disappeared. Feeling very annoyed, he walked back to the narrowboat and explained what had happened. They moored the boat and started to clean up the mess with a few buckets of water.

The three responsible for this mayhem had meanwhile left the scene and headed across the fields for the next bridge, but in the opposite direction to the boat they had just bombarded and they were laughing at the way, the prank had gone so successfully.

Meanwhile, Gorrin was continuing to walk along the canal whistling a merry tune to keep him company, when he heard the sound of another boat chugging along the canal. It was coming from behind him and he looked around as it drew nearer. This boat was different to the other ones he had seen, as this one seemed to have no living quarters in the middle. There were what appeared to be two cabins, one at the front of the boat and one at the rear, where the man steering the boat was currently standing.

The boat chugged past and Gorrin turned to look at the boat and realised why there was no cabin in the middle, - it was a working cargo-carrying boat. He studied the boat and noticed that one of the storage holds was covered with a tent, while the second one was completely open to the weather.

Brian was the owner of the narrowboat and was listening to music as it went past Gorrin. When the boat drew level with the figure on the towpath, he noticed that the small child looking at him was not a child at all, but a short man with a silvery grey beard and a green tunic and green trousers, with shiny black boots. He also noticed that he was wearing a pointed green hat and had bright blue eyes that seemed to twinkle.

Gorrin smiled at Brian and so Brian smiled back and nodded his head and mouthed "Good Morning" to the unusual little man, as the noise of the diesel engine made it difficult to hear what anyone on the canal side said. He looked back at the small person while his boat continued on along the canal towards his destination of Stratford-upon-Avon.

As the dark blue painted canal boat had slowly moved past Gorrin, he had noticed that the name on the side of the boat said 'Round Tuit'. Gorrin continued to walk pondering on the strange name for a short while, watching a small family of coots with their distinctive black and red markings paddling along near the far bank. By the time his attention had reverted back to the boat in front, he noticed that it was some distance away and approaching a bridge.

James, Simon and Sarah had, by this time, reached the next canal bridge and had already spotted their next target slowly coming towards their hiding place behind the bridge parapet. Giggling James opened the plastic bag of soggy tomatoes and passed them around. Unfortunately for Simon, the tomato he picked up was so soggy it split and ran down the back of his hand. Grinning he flicked it at Sarah, but Sarah was having none of this so she threw hers at Simon. It missed and flew over the top of the parapet to land in the canal.

Meanwhile Brian's boat moved ever closer to the bridge where the three were hiding. He noticed something red fly over the top of the bridge and land in the water with an odd splash. As the boat started to pass under the bridge, three heads popped up over the bridge and this was followed by several soggy tomatoes.

Brian was not too bothered by this as he had been witness to a range of different missiles coming from bridges, from shopping trolleys to even old golf umbrellas. That was, until the stink bombs started landing and then splat! One of the tomatoes had landed right on his head and the cold juice was now running down the back of his neck, along with all of the tomato pips.

Gnomes have exceptionally good eyesight and Gorrin had been half watching the scene when he became aware of the sudden bombardment of red missiles down on to the canal boat that had recently passed him. He frowned as he realised that something was happening and that this something was not good. When the soggy tomato hit the boatman and splattered, Gorrin had to smile, as it did look funny, but when another tomato hit the poor boatman he stopped himself smiling and decided that he was going to intervene.

Gorrin took out of his pocket the purple velvet pouch and took a pinch of the glittering powder; he quickly replaced the pouch and threw the powder into the air, muttering a little verse as he did so. Pop! Gorrin vanished suddenly and reappeared on the bridge behind where the three children were now standing as they continued to throw tomatoes and stink bombs at the canal boat below.

Gorrin immediately rubbed the stone on his ring and he faded from view. He quickly moved over to where James was standing and snatched the bag away from him. James turned around to see the bag floating in the air and it seemed to fade like mist until it could not be seen.

He could not believe what he was seeing and his mouth opened wide in surprise.

"Look at that," he said to Simon and Sarah.

"Look at what?" said Simon.

"The bag of tomatoes just vanished!" exclaimed James.

"What are you talking about? Sarah asked, "Bags don't just disappear."

"Well this one did," said James.

Just then, the first of the missing soggy tomatoes appeared in mid air and hit Simon on the chest and spattered all over his clothes. This was followed by another tomato that hit James on the head splat! One tomato hit Sarah on the leg. Then, one after another of the tomatoes, headed in their direction, to spatter all three from head to foot. Gorrin started to laugh as he ran out of soggy tomatoes.

This was too much for the three practical jokers as the joke was now on them and they all started to run away from the bridge and head home as fast as their legs could carry them.

As they headed off the bridge all they could hear was a strange laughing that seemed to come out of thin air, but they were not about to stop and see whom it was, that was laughing, as they were too scared.

Just as the three ran off, the boatman who had moored his boat by the side of the bridge had climbed up the canal bank on to the bridge. He quickly realised, that the three who had bombarded him had themselves become targets, as they were now covered with the remains of soggy tomatoes.

Brian started to laugh himself when he understood that the tables had been turned on the three practical jokers, until suddenly in front of him a small figure shimmered into view. Immediately he recognised the little man as the same one that had smiled at him earlier, but he was completely surprised by his sudden re-appearance.

Gorrin watched the retreating three jokers and turned around to face the boatman who had just appeared at the other end of the bridge and had started to laugh. He rubbed the ring and the invisibility fell away from him. "Good morrow Sir, Do not be afraid," Gorrin, said to the boatman, "I'm a friend."

At first the boatman was too surprised to speak, and the strange way that this small man spoke was odd to say the least, but eventually he managed to say "Er. Yes. Er. Thanks, thanks very much."

"My great pleasure," said Gorrin.

"I owe you one," said Brian.

"Well, now you mention it, perhaps there is something that you can do for me", said Gorrin.

"Pray, tell me, where are you headed for?

Brian replied, "Stratford-upon-Avon. I have a load of building stone to deliver for the Council."

"Perhaps you can let me ride in your boat then?" queried Gorrin.

"Well I will be glad of the company," Brian replied, "It can get a bit lonely sometimes on the cut."

"The cut what?" Gorrin said.

"No," chuckled Brian, "The 'cut' is another name for the canal."

"Oh!" remarked Gorrin. "Anyhow, I am forgetting my manners. My name is Gorrin. To whom do I have the pleasure of addressing?"

"My name is Brian," he replied. "Pleased to meet you Gorrin."

Brian considered that this rather unusual small character spoke in a very strange way. It sounded like old English, but his knowledge of history was limited. He dismissed such thoughts from his mind and looked hard at this newcomer. After a moment he walked forward and they both shook hands.

After a moment both carefully scrambled down the canal bank back to the boat and Brian climbed on board quickly followed by Gorrin.

"Follow Me," said Brian, "We'll have a nice cup of tea."

"What is tea?" said Gorrin.

"Oh, have you never had a cup of tea? Brian asked.

"No," said Gorrin. "What is it made from?"

Brian paused briefly before replying, and then said, "Dried tea leaves, milk and sugar and, of course, water."

"Erm... What is sugar?" asked Gorrin

Brian thought to himself, "I wonder where he's from and where he's been, not to know about sugar." Brian continued, "It's used to sweeten drinks and other things."

"Oh!" exclaimed Gorrin again, and then he smiled, "It must be like the honey I use to sweeten drinks at home."

"And where is that?" enquired Brian.

So Gorrin, started to tell Brian his story about how he been woken up by the yellow smelly machine. As Gorrin told his story, Brian's eyes grew wider and wider and his expression became more and more astonished.

Brian poured two cups of hot sweet tea and passed one to Gorrin.

"Careful" said Brian, "It's very hot."

"Mmm" said Gorrin, "That is a very nice drink".

Then, Gorrin continued to tell the story. Gorrin was very quick at picking up language and he rapidly started to speak in a similar way to Brian although the odd word lapsed back into old English. In a strange and different world, it was going to be very important not to stand out any more than he had to and language was a key way in which to blend in.

Time passed quickly and eventually Brian realised that so much time had passed by, that if he wasn't careful, he would be late in delivering his load of decorative stone. Apologising that he must cut the conversation short, as he needed to continue his journey, Brian climbed out of the small cabin and up on to the rear deck of the narrowboat.

He started up the boat engine and as it jumped into life, the vessel shuddered and the engine started chugging. Then Brian jumped on to the canal bank, removed the mooring rope from the steel stake that was securing the boat to the canal bank, then he jumped back on board and the boat then slowly moved off from the canal bank.

Soon the narrowboat was chugging steadily along at a steady speed and passed a number of brick bridges and a number of lift bridges. The lift bridges had to be raised by the use of a winding handle. Eventually the boat reached the Kingswood junction at Lapworth. Here, there were a large number of locks to get through.

Gorrin had never seen canal locks before, and was very interested in seeing how they operated. He thought it was very clever how the water was either raised or lowered, to allow the boat to go up or down hills. The lock gates reminded him of wooden castle gates, but where castle gates took many men to open and close them, one person could open the lock gates.

As the "Round Tuit" travelled down the lock system, they passed a number of boats travelling in the opposite direction. Gorrin decided, after being stared at by quite a number of boatmen and 'Gongoozlers,' to stay out of sight, and so he decided to use his magic ring.

Before Gorrin used the magic ring however, he warned Brian about what he intended to do, so that he did not worry about where he was. As Gorrin shimmered out of sight, Brian was still a little perturbed to hear Gorrin's voice appear out of thin air, but he eventually got used to this strange disembodied voice appearing in front of him.

He had one question that he just had to ask and so Gorrin said, "Brian, what is a Gongoozler?"

"That's easy," said Brian. "Its just anyone who looks on at what the boats are doing on the canal, but does not offer to help, particularly when you are going through the locks".

"Oh!" Exclaimed Gorrin, "My, that is a very strange name."

As they continued the conversation, Brian was not aware at first that other boaters were looking at him strangely, as he continued to have a conversation with the now invisible Gorrin. They continued to travel through the Kingswood Junction and Brian noticed a number of children on one boat pointing at him and laughing. They even shouted out to him, calling him a mad boatman who talked to himself.

At this point, Brian realised that he must indeed look as though he was having a serious conversation with himself, so he became more careful when talking to Gorrin. And so time passed uneventfully and they slowly made their way down through the numerous locks.

At the end of the day they were through the Kingswood Junction and by the time it was getting dusk, they were both hungry. The hunger was not surprising, since they had both missed their midday meal because Gorrin had been relating his story to Brian.

Once well past the main group of locks, Brian found a nice quiet stretch of canal and moored the boat for the night. Now the boat was secure, Brian started to cook the evening meal.

The evening meal was a simple one of bacon, sausage, eggs, mushrooms and tomatoes and when the tomatoes were served up, both started to laugh at the event earlier in the day.

"I won't forget the look on their three faces for a long time," chucked Brian. "It was worth getting hit on the head with a mushy tomato, just to see that."

Gorrin continued to tell his story as the dusk outside quickly changed to night and the air went much cooler. "That was a delicious meal," said Gorrin, But I have never tasted tomatoes before." Then they both laughed again.

After they had cleared away all the dirty plates and washed them up. Gorrin was tired after the two days events and needed a good night's rest in a proper bed. He told Brian that he needed to get some sleep and said goodnight. Gorrin stepped through the cabin door on to the cargo deck, under the canvas tent. Brian wished him a good night's sleep and closed the door.

Gorrin sniffed the air as he carefully picked his way to the small cabin at the front of the boat. Brian had told Gorrin that he had a spare cabin at the front of his boat and that he was welcome to use it. Gorrin gratefully accepted. The cold air signalled the start of the autumn frosts, thought Gorrin, Oh well, not to worry. At least he had somewhere warm and dry to sleep.

Gorrin changed into his nightgown and put on his spare nightcap, drew back the bed covers then climbed into bed. He closed his eyes and he thought about the events of the day and promising himself that he must write them up in his journal the following day. With these thoughts wafting through his mind he drifted off to sleep.

~~~~~~~~~~~~~~~~~~~~~~~~~~~~~

Chapter Five
"The Canal Breach"

The sun rose and started to break through the early morning mist that lay over the canal, Gorrin was awoken by the dawn chorus of the birds in the trees at the side of the canal. For a few seconds he could not remember where he was, then as he became more aware of his surroundings, his recollection of the previous day's events came back to him. He sat up and looked around the small cabin, the light of the morning slipping through the small curtain that partly covered the little round window on the side of the boat.

Pulling back the bed covers, he took off his nightcap and got out of bed and began to make himself ready for the day. He found that there was a small washing bowl that lay in a metal sink made of some strange shiny metal. The washing bowl itself was also unusual from Gorrin's point of view as he had never seen or held plastic before.

Studying the two strange metal bent tubes that were adjacent to the sink, he realised that this must be a tap. Yesterday when he had helped Brian to wash up, after the evening meal, he had noticed that this strange device was a much smaller version of his own sink faucet. He turned the blue coloured tap on and the cold water flowed out into the bowl. For a short while he played a little game turning the tap on and off, marvelling at the way it responded to his efforts.

Eventually he grew bored with this little game and just let it continue to fill the washing bowl until it was half full. At this point he turned off the blue tap and turned on the red tap. Cold water spurted out of this tap for a few moments then the water gradually got warmer and warmer, until it was piping hot. As the steam from the hot water rose into the cabin, he was fascinated at how easy it was to produce a seemly never-ending stream of hot water so quickly, without the use of magic.

Once the bowl was full, he started to wash and prepare himself for the day and a short while later he was washed and dressed. He unpacked his quill, ink and parchment journal and set about writing up the previous day's events. By the time he had finished and was ready to go the sun had started to climb its way into the sky.

Outside the cabin, the early morning mist was now beginning to rise and clear as the sun continued its climb into the sky. Gorrin picked up his backpack, blackthorn staff and went out on to the deck and carefully walked along the edge of the deck. He looked at the cargo of decorative stone that the narrowboat was carrying. Puzzled, he examined the stone that was encased in a large net bag made of similar strange material to the washing bowl. Of course Gorrin had never seen plastic and he resolved to discuss this with Brian at the earliest opportunity.

Gorrin approached Brian's cabin at the stern of the boat and became aware of the sound of movement within. He politely knocked on the cabin door and then opened the door when he heard Brian say, "Come in Gorrin, did you sleep well?"

Gorrin replied "Yes thank you Brian, that was a most wonderful bed, in fact it was one of the most comfortable I have ever slept in."

"Oh!" said Brian, "It's nothing special."

While the conversation continued, Brian set about preparing a hot pot of tea. He put some bacon in a frying pan, with some button mushrooms and started to put out two cereal bowls on the sink unit. "I always believe you should start the day with a good breakfast" Brian said, "It sets you up for the day."

Gorrin agreed and added "My dear old mother used to say, breakfast as a King, lunch as a Prince and evening meal as a pauper."

"That's a phrase I have not heard in a long time" said Brian. "Now", said Brian "What sort of cereal to you want?"

Gorrin didn't know what Brian meant until he looked over to where Brian was pointing and saw two small boxes with brightly coloured pictures on the cover, with very strange words on the box. One box said "Malt Pieces", while the other one said "Cornflakes".

Gorrin did not have any idea which to choose, so he said, "Which one are you going to have Brian?"

Brian studied the boxes for a few seconds then said "The cornflakes, as I quite fancy them with a spot of very cold milk."

Gorrin thought about this for a moment, but since he did not have any idea what they were decided to have the same as Brian.

Brian had, meanwhile, pulled the table out from its storage point at the side of the cabin and then placed the two cereal bowls on, together with the now full teapot. As they settled down at the small table in the cabin, Brian poured the cornflakes into the two bowls. He had already placed the carton of milk from the refrigerator on to the table, so he picked up the milk carton and poured it over the cereal.

They settled down to eat, the sound of the frying bacon and mushrooms sizzling in the frying pan could be heard as it crackled, while the aroma wafted around the small cabin. This was one of the most pleasant smells that he had smelt in the morning for a long time, thought Gorrin.

Gorrin ate the cornflakes and cold milk with the spoon, he thought how clean tasting the cold milk and cereal was - quite unlike anything that he had ever tasted before. Once the cereal was eaten, Brian had taken the cooked bacon and mushrooms out of the pan and placed them on to four slices of bread. He quickly made two sandwiches, one each for Gorrin and himself.

The bacon and mushroom 'butties', as Brian called them, were absolutely delicious, and while Gorrin finished eating, he felt the remaining hunger pangs fading away. The tea was quickly poured into two large tin mugs and they both sat back for a few moments to enjoy the sun that was now streaming though the small round window in the cabin.

Breakfast over, Brian rose up and went out on to the rear deck to start the engine. As the engine started up it made a strange clunking sound, before it suddenly started running properly, This was accompanied by a blast of sooty smoke that shot upwards and seemed to hang briefly in the cold morning air before lazily drifting away.

Just before the engine had fired up, Gorrin had heard the sound of some mallard ducks quacking, but as he peered into the rapidly clearing mist, in spite of his good eyesight, he was not able to spot where the sound had come from.

Now the engine was started and running properly, Brian, jumped on to the canal bank and quickly removed the mooring spikes and rope, then quickly returned to the boat. As soon as he reached the boat helm where the rudder was located, he engaged the forward gear and slowly the boat edged forward from the bank into the mid point of the canal.

Gorrin peered into the mist in front of the boat as it continued to move forward, and settled down to a comfortable ride to the next canal lock. The South Stratford canal that they were now on is one of the most heavily locked stretches of canal on the canal system. Brian had explained that from the Kings Norton top lock, there were fifty-five locks to get through. Fortunately for Gorrin, they had only thirty-one more locks to go, before they reached Stratford.

It was only a short while before the first of the day's locks was reached and so began the long process of 'locking through'. While getting though a canal lock when you are single handed taking a boat though canal locks is possible, it was always hard work.

Gorrin had been watching Brian closely how he operated the locks, and after a couple more locks, he resolved to help Brian to get through the locks as quickly as possible. In order to help Brian get through the locks, Gorrin decided to use a little magic to help things along

This needed a very special and sensitive type of magic, and he needed to use his staff. But first he had to consult a very special old book of ancient magic. Since this book was very old and very special and contained many hundreds of spells, it was also capable of causing a great deal of mischief in the wrong hands.

In order to protect the book, it had protective charms in place to guard it. If you tried to pick it up without saying the first charm, the book would just tend to slip out of your hands. The second protection charm on the book, was the book lock, and this needed a special key to operate it. The key was the amethyst stone in Gorrin's invisibility ring and it had to be placed in the centre of the lock, while singing the unlock charm.

Even if you managed to get through those two protection charms, there was a third and final charm. If you failed to sing the final charm, when the book was opened, all that anyone would see would be a lot of blank pages. If the final charm had been sung however, then the words on the pages would appear and the book could then be studied.

Gorrin had already disarmed the three protection charms and was now reading though the book. When he found what he was looking for he read and memorised the charm and then closed the book. With the book closed, the lock automatically shut and the protection charms self set into place.

He replaced the book back into his jacket inside pocket and picked up his staff, as he did so he sang in a very soft manner to the staff, pointing it at the sluice gate handles at the side of the lock gate. As he did this the runes on the staff glowed a very pale yellow colour and a pale yellow light started to stream away from the end of the staff towards the sluice gate handle. As the light struck the device, the sluice gate opened and the water started to flow out of the lock and into the downstream side of the lock and into the lock pound itself.

Brian suddenly realised that the lock was emptying quite quickly and then he heard Gorrin's voice telling him not to worry as Gorrin was responsible for this and that he was trying to help by speeding things along. The first lock that Gorrin tried this was very slow, but quickly Brian and Gorrin learnt to work together and pretty soon, things were going very well.

That was until they reached lock 34. Just as they were approaching a small aqueduct that ran over a small stream, there was a strange noise coming from the aqueduct itself.

The strange noise increased in volume as they approached, until it became obvious that all was not right. They could both hear the sound of water cascading out of the canal and down into the stream below. There had been a canal breach and if things weren't sorted out pretty quickly, the entire section of canal could end up draining out through the hole. This would give everyone travelling on the canal a problem, as well as the farmers' animals on the low-lying land around the breach.

Brian, once he realised the problem, spoke to Gorrin. Knowing that Gorrin was able to use magic, he asked him if he was able to repair the damage, before the entire section of canal became drained. Gorrin thought quickly and said to Brian, "I need to be able to get down to the side of the hole so I can use my staff and repair the breach."

"OK" Brian replied, and with that the narrowboat was quickly steered towards the towpath.

As soon as the boat reached the bank, Gorrin jumped off and landed with a little bump on the path. Running along as fast as his little legs could carry him; he reached the aqueduct and carefully climbed down the bank. When he was in a better position to see the extent of the damage, Gorrin realised he would have to work fast or the entire section of bank would give way. If that happened the low lying land would of course be flooded, but more to the point, all of the canal boats on that part of the canal, would be stranded, including, of course, Brian and himself.

As fast as he was able, Gorrin opened the green velvet pouch, then took out a pinch of the strange powder inside and threw it over the breach, muttering a little song at the same time. A few seconds later, soil, rocks and clay rose up and started to block the hole, however the torrent of water was just too fast for this gentle magic to have any real effect.

Gorrin quickly understood that the problem was just too large for this type of magic - it needed something a lot less subtle. He sprinted back to the narrowboat, and when Brian asked him if he had managed to seal the hole, Gorrin answered, "No Brian, but I am going to try something else." He then picked up his staff from the boat deck and then jumped back on to the bank and finally ran back down the bank.

As he had been running back to the boat to collect his staff, the hole in the bank grew even wider and this was now starting to cause quite a current flow in the canal. So much so, that Brian's boat was being pulled towards the hole. Brian had just realised this and had increased the engine speed and engaged the drive to try to move the boat out of harms way, since the stretch of the canal they were now on, was beginning to show signs that its level was starting to drop more and more.

Gorrin reached the canal breach and pointed his staff at the torrent of water and started to sing very softly at first, but as the song went on, his voice increased in volume. As he sang, the runes on the staff had started to pulse a purple colour. A purple light shot out of the end of the staff and wherever the light came into contact, the soil, boulders, stones, trees and wild flowers were scooped up and then headed for the water torrent.

Crash! Splash! The noise of all this material crashing down into the torrent of water was very loud and at first the amount of material hardly affected the flow outwards at all. But still Gorrin continued his song and so more and more mud, stones and other debris headed towards the breach in the canal bank.

After a couple of minutes, the mass of material Gorrin had aimed at the water torrent had slowed the torrent to a small trickle. Eventually the hole was sealed, and not a moment too soon. As Gorrin looked around at the mass of mud and rock, he spotted a number of other cracks running from the hole. He continued to repair all the damage he could with the use of his runic staff, the strange purple light playing over the area.

Brian had by this time, managed to moor the narrowboat a good distance from the breach and had ran back along the towpath to where Gorrin was standing. As he gazed at the scene, he understood that this little silvery grey haired gnome had prevented a minor disaster.

"Good work Gorrin!" Brian almost shouted this. He was very much relieved that Gorrin had managed to seal the breach, for obvious reasons. He could not afford to be late delivering the stone, as he could lose money on the contract if he was delayed.

"No problem... at least, not now," replied Gorrin.

By now, there was little evidence that a major canal breach had taken place, apart from the obvious issues of mud and water that had actually flowed down into the surrounding countryside. Finally, when Gorrin was fully satisfied with the repair, he closed the charm and the staff runes faded back to lie dormant and quiet, until they would be needed again. Gorrin studied the waterlogged fields and decided that there was little he could do to rectify such extensive damage, so he shrugged his shoulders and climbed back up the embankment.

They both walked back to the boat. Brian said that he needed a good cup of tea, and Gorrin promptly agreed. Once back in the boat they both sat down in the little cabin at the rear or stern of the canal boat, while the kettle on the stove heated.

"That was a close run thing," said Gorrin.

"You can say that again," said Brian.

"That was a close run thing!" said Gorrin.

Brian looked over at Gorrin to see if he was joking, to see the beginnings of a smile playing around the corner of his mouth. As he looked closer, Brian's stare caused Gorrin to burst out laughing, as he said "Well, I nearly got you there!" Brian then started to laugh himself.

After they had both drunk their much-needed tea, and eaten the biscuits that Brian had opened, they both went back outside to continue their journey toward Stratford-upon-Avon.

"This canal journey was proving to be quite an adventure in its own right," thought Gorrin, "I wonder just what will happen next."

~~~~~~~~~~~~~~~~~~~~~~~~~

Chapter Six
"Arrival at Stratford-upon-Avon"

With all of the various events happening Gorrin had forgotten to ask Brian a key question, and so as the boat chugged along the canal he decided to ask it. "Brian, what year is it?"

"Oh, it's 2005, why?" Brian replied.

Gorrin was stunned and sat down on a step with a thump.

He had not realised that he had been asleep for so long. He thought it was quite a long time, but more than three hundred and fifty years! That took some swallowing at no mistake, he thought.

"Are you all right Gorrin?" Brian asked. Although he could not see Gorrin, as Gorrin was once again invisible, he had heard the sound of Gorrin landing with a thump on the step.

"I must have a made a mistake in the charm when I put myself to sleep," said Gorrin, "And a big mistake at that" he continued.

"How long have you been asleep then Gorrin?" asked Brian.

"Three hundred and fifty years, give or take a few," replied Gorrin.

"What?" exclaimed Brian, "That's incredible!"

Gorrin was very quiet at this point and Brian looked over to where the thought Gorrin was sitting.

"I wonder what has become of my family, in all that time." Gorrin said. "I never thought I had been out for that length of time - a few years, maybe a hundred or so at most." He paused for a few seconds then said, "I suppose that I knew deep down that it was much longer, but I didn't want to believe it. What with all these machines and strange words everyone seems to use."

Brian looked thoughtfully into space as he tried to put himself in Gorrin's shoes. With a quick calculation he worked it out that it must have been at least 1660. Gorrin said "Well actually Brian it was just about1650."

He looked back at where Gorrin was and said "Gorrin, if my history is correct, that was well before the Great Fire of London that happened in 1666."

Gorrin looked up to where Brian was standing and said, "What fire, Brian?"

Brian replied; "Well, as I seem to remember from my school history lessons, the 'Great Fire of London' started in a bakers and the street was called Pudding Lane. I think most of London was destroyed at the time, but it eventually burnt itself out. I can't remember any details though." Brian paused again before continuing, "But the city was rebuilt and ended up a much better city as a result."

"Well that's good," said Gorrin. "Anyway, none of my family lived in London, as we Gnomes don't like towns and cities much, as they tend to be dirty smelly places."

"Well," said Brian, "Nothing much has changed with the cities, they are still dirty and smelly, but from cars and trucks rather than sewers!"

"Hmm" said Gorrin. "What are cars and trucks?" he asked.

"They are vehicles Gorrin," said Brian. "The cars are used by ordinary people while the trucks are used to transport goods."

"They must be like the horse drawn carts we used," said Gorrin.

For a little while the conversation continued, until they reached the next lock and then Brian and Gorrin began 'locking through' with Gorrin helping using his magic as before.

Once through this lock they carried on to the next. They continued on for a couple more hours, gradually drawing nearing to Stratford-upon-Avon. In the breaks between locks, the conversation continued.

"Brian," enquired Gorrin another thing I have been meaning to ask you. Your boat has a very strange name, 'Round Tuit', what does it mean?"

Brian smiled, then said "It's a joke Gorrin, before I started life on the canals, I used to be in the armed services and my mates always used to make fun, in a good natured way, of me saying that I would get around to it, so I thought that I would have a joke on them and call it 'Round Tuit." Gorrin looked thoughtful at first, then as he understood the joke he started to laugh while he repeated "I'll get a round to it…Round Tuit, Oh yes that's very good Brian."

"Well," said Brian. "At least you are laughing again."

Gorrin responded by saying, "Yes, thanks Brian, I was feeling more than a little sad and lonely at the news, as it was such a shock. I think I am fine now, but more than ever, I want to find out what has become of my family, after all those years."

They had reached another set of locks and this bought the conversation to a halt as they had to go through, as a boat was waiting to come up through the locks, so to conserve water, they had to take a lock full of water with them, to prevent a full lock of water being wasted.

Once through the lock Brian said that they should have a break, as it was now nearly lunchtime. Gorrin thought that this was a good idea and so they both descended into the cabin to make their lunch. The day was now warm and sunny, after the sun had slowly burnt all the mist away, Brian suggested that he make sandwiches and Gorrin liked the sound of that, but didn't know what Brian meant so he asked him.

"Sorry, I keep forgetting that there is a lot of what I take for granted that you have no knowledge of Gorrin," said Brian. And so Brian explained what a sandwich was and how it was made. Gorrin listened intently, as food was one of his favourite topics of conversation.

The sandwiches Brian made were cheese and pickle and ham and tomato. As Brian sliced the tomatoes, he looked across at Gorrin and winked. Gorrin smiled as he remembered the incident with the tomatoes on the bridge, the previous day.

With a mug of hot sweet tea each and the sandwiches, they both sat and relaxed as they ate their lunch.

"These are delicious," exclaimed Gorrin as he munched on the sandwiches. "And so easy to make," he said.

"Glad you like them," Brian replied.

Once the lunch was eaten and the plates and mugs washed and dried, Brian headed back up on to the deck and started the engine. The engine was now running smoothly and he stepped on to the towpath and released the narrowboat from its moorings, retrieving the mooring spikes as he did so. Stepping back on to the boat, they continued their journey down through the various locks.

As they progressed through the beautiful countryside, Gorrin watched mallard ducks and coots paddling along on the far bank, in and out of the weeds and bulrushes, whilst he listed to their calls. Several times as they progressed along the South Stratford canal, he had seen a heron and even the occasional dragonfly, with its shimmering colours on its long body, as it darted over the water.

As the boat chugged through the water, Gorrin found the way the bow wave spread out from the front hypnotic and very relaxing. He really did enjoy this type of life, that was a nice steady pace – not too fast and not too slow. He was eventually disturbed out of his thoughts by Brian calling his name.

"Gorrin…. Gorrin…." Brian called. "We are approaching Preston Bagot – that's not very far from Stratford."

Gorrin stood up and looked forwards towards the steel split bridges that lay across the canal and the unusual 'Barrel Cottages' that were beside the locks. These cottages were so named due to their strange barrel shaped roof. They continued on through the flight of locks and Gorrin looked at the wooded area that lay each side of the canal and thought that it was very pretty, as it lay so far away from the hustle and bustle of towns and cities.

Once through this set of locks there was another stretch of canal that was without locks and Gorrin welcomed this, as he was beginning to get a little tired of getting wet every time they went through these quite old lock chambers. The chambers were built of old engineering bricks and because of their age, they were porous so that as the water level dropped and the boat descended, water would start to cascade on to him from above through the holes in the brickwork. The result was that he had got wet numerous times and was more than a little annoyed that his nice green tunic was wet and covered in spatters of mud.

They crossed another aqueduct, and Gorrin looked anxiously at it, but he did not have to worry as this particular one was in good order. He noticed that it was made of some sort of metal and crossed a road. As he looked down at the road, he noticed wheeled vehicles that Brian called cars, moving along at what was a very fast pace on the road. They were in brightly painted colours and he could see the people inside them as they passed underneath the aqueduct.

Brian informed him that they were now at Wootton Wawen. The boat continued onwards through more locks and more miles of canal, and they eventually reached Wilmcote. It was during this last series of locks that became Gorrin startled by a very loud noise and quickly raised his staff. He was ready to fight the strange monster that was now charging along beside the canal.

Studying the new intruder, Gorrin quickly realised that this was another machine and it moved on rails of metal. It quickly passed them and once the noise had subsided, Brian informed Gorrin that it was a train. He listened to Brian, explained all he knew concerning these large and noisy monsters, while he returned to helping the narrowboat through the canal locks.

Gorrin was amazed at how anything so large could move at such a speed, but then he was getting used to all the many changes that had occurred in the years he had been asleep. The train had rushed past and he had observed the many faces at the windows.

Gorrin mentioned this to Brian, who at first did not understand what his friend meant. The gnome continued to explain that when he had last been journeying the countryside, there had been far fewer people around.

The miles on the canal were gradually completed until they eventually reached the Stratford-upon-Avon marina. This was the destination of Brian and it was here that the cargo of stone was to be unloaded. Brian carefully manoeuvred the boat alongside the quay close to the lifting cranes and the slipway. Once the boat was secured against the mooring rings, Brian told Gorrin that he had to find the man from the council, whom he was supposed to meet.

While Brian was meeting the man from the council, Gorrin suggested that he make them both a nice cup of tea, to which Brian agreed that this was a good idea. As an afterthought, Brian asked Gorrin if he was okay with the gas stove and kettle. Gorrin, being Gorrin of course, said "Yes Brian, that shouldn't be a problem." Brian stared at Gorrin for a couple of seconds then nodded and added, "I shouldn't be too long." And with that, Brian walked away towards the boat office.

Gorrin looked at the gas stove and the kettle with a degree of concern, as he had never actually used them on the boat before. He removed the lid of the kettle and looked inside and decided that it needed more water so using the tap he added more water. Now the kettle was full, he placed it upon the stove. This was tricky moment he thought, now to light the gas!

He looked around for the matches that Brian had used earlier and found them on a little shelf at the side of the sink. He opened the box and looked inside. There were only two matches left, "Oh dear" said Gorrin out loud, "I will have to make sure that these work properly." He walked over to the stove and struck one of the matches, but the end broke off and fell on to the floor. "Rats! I didn't mean to do that", said Gorrin, a little annoyed that things had not gone according to plan.

He tried again with the last remaining match in the box; it flared up, the flame sputtering as it did so. Unfortunately for Gorrin, as he turned the gas on, the match went out.

"Rats again! exclaimed Gorrin, "This is getting tiresome. Now, how am I going to light the stove?" He stood and thought for a few moments, a frown settling across his face. "Of course!" he said out loud. He walked across to where he had left his runic staff and picked it up. Turning around he pointed the staff at the gas cooker hob and started to sing in his ancient language.

The runes glowed red and a thin red light shot out of the end of the staff. WHUMPH! Gorrin did not understand about gas and had left the gas tap on. Fortunately for Gorrin, only a few seconds had passed, but this was enough for some of the gas to accumulate around the top of the cooker and, of course, this had ignited with the red light from the staff.

Gorrin staggered back as the flash of heat hit him. The small explosion has caused soot from the cooker to be blown into the air and the heat had singed his eyebrows, hair and beard. There were now smuts of soot liberally covering his face and clothes and he looked as if he had been sweeping the chimney. Dust and soot was hanging in the air and covering the surfaces of much of the small kitchen. He gazed on the scene and said "What a mess! Brian is not going to be very pleased with this at all."

He walked over to the cooker and placed the kettle on to the now burning gas ring to boil. Then Gorrin lifted out of his tunic pocket, the green velvet pouch and took a small pinch of the glittering powder inside. He threw this pinch into the air whilst at the same time singing the little charm. The air seemed to sparkle with green twinkling stars and quickly all of the surfaces covered in soot and dust were cleaned, until the entire kitchen seemed to sparkle. It was the cleanest it had ever looked in all of its years.

At that moment, Gorrin heard Brian climbing back on board the narrowboat and then coming down the stairwell into the kitchen. As Brian entered, he caught sight of Gorrin and he stopped in his tracks. The little gnome was covered head to foot in soot and smuts, both on his clothes and his face. It was obvious to him that his eyebrows and beard were scorched. Brian looked past the gnome and saw that the kitchen was cleaner than he had ever seen it.

Brian looked back at Gorrin, who was looking at him with an innocent "Who me?" look that clearly indicated he had done something that he was embarrassed about. Brian started to laugh at the sight and Gorrin, realising that Brian was not angry started to laugh as well.

"Well?" asked Brian, who was still trying not to laugh too much, "What happened?"

Gorrin explained to Brian, and as he related the story, Brian continued looking around for signs of damage, but could see none.

While Gorrin was explaining how things had gone a little haywire, the kettle started to whistle, Brian walked over to the stove and finished making the tea. Gorrin, meanwhile, had walked over to the mirror and was now looking at his own reflection. Looking back at him was a gnome in a very sorry state indeed.

His lovely silvery grey beard was now covered in soot and had been scorched away at the edges, together with his eyebrows. As he continued to gaze, he understood that he had just had a very lucky escape indeed. He resolved to be much more careful in future with the gas cooker.

He took another pinch of the green powder out of the green velvet pouch and sprinkled it over himself and uttered the special charm. He was covered head to foot in twinkling stars and then all the soot and smut vanished. The only sign that things were not quite what they were before the accident, was the look on his face!

Gorrin turned round to face Brian and walked over to a seat and sat down at the little table, meanwhile, Brian had poured the two mugs of hot sweet tea and placed them on to the table.

Brian had been watching Gorrin as he had used the magic powder on himself and had raised an eyebrow as the magic had repaired the physical damage. He could see however, from the startled look on Gorrin's face, that the accident had shaken the little gnome. Poor Gorrin, he thought.

As they drank their tea, Brian changed the subject of conversation to the boatyard. He explained that there was no council official at the yard at the moment and that there would not be until late tomorrow morning, so they were going to have to wait until then. In the meantime, it was time for their evening meal, so as they continued to talk, Brian set about making it.

While Brian prepared the meal, Gorrin gathered together his writing materials and began writing up the day's events in his journal. Brian was fascinated at how Gorrin used the quill pen, ink and parchment to write about the day's events. Just as he finished writing, Brian announced he was ready to serve the evening meal.

Brian put spaghetti on to the two plates and followed this with the Bolognese sauce topping and then sat down to eat it with Gorrin. As they ate, Brian poured Gorrin a glass of red wine and raised his glass to Gorrin and made a toast, "Cheers Gorrin, I hope you find your family."

Gorrin raised his glass also and responded by saying, "Cheer's Brian, thank-you for your kindness in letting me travel with you."

The conversation continued on as the darkness outside closed in around the boat, until Gorrin announced that he was quite tired and thought he had better go to bed.

With that, Gorrin got up and wished Brian a goodnight and retired to his cabin. As he walked to his cabin, he looked up at the twinkling stars in the night sky. As he studied the stars he thought to himself that while the world around seemed to have changed a lot, at least some things had not changed. With that final thought for the day, he retired to bed.

~~~~~~~~~~~~~~~~~~~~~~

Chapter Seven
"The Boat Yard"

Gorrin was normally a light sleeper but during the night Gorrin was awoken by strange sounds wafting in though the open window. The strange noises were coming from the boatyard. The sound that had awoken him first, was the noise of glass breaking and this made him sit bolt upright with a start.

He listened carefully and waited for more noises. As he listened Gorrin became aware of hushed voices talking and from the sound of them, they belonged to two men. He quickly got out of bed as silently as he could and picked up his staff and slowly and quietly opened the cabin door.

A few moments earlier, two young men had entered the boatyard with the aim of stealing cash, and anything else of value they could lay their hands on. They were both dressed in dark clothing and were used to this kind of work. As they approached the office building they were having a hushed conversation.

"Hey Lee, this is your bright idea. You sure there'll be cash in the till?" whispered Kevin.

"Course I am. Look, I overheard that guy in the pub talking the other night about how the old man sometimes can't be bothered to clear it out some nights, so there's bound to be cash there," retorted Lee.

"Alright keep your 'air on, I was just askin' that's all," answered Kevin.

"Huh!" grunted Lee back.

"Anyway, how come there's no alarm?" persisted Lee.

"Look, how many times do I have to tell you, the old man who owns the place had an alarm fitted but the old skinflint bought a cheap one and its knackered and he's waiting to have a better one fitted, OK?"

"Yeh, I spose," Kevin replied.

Lee hugged the shadows cast by the office from the street lamps opposite and slid up to the window. He wrapped a roll of material around his fist and arm and tapped the glass with the small hammer he had just removed from one of his deep pockets. The glass cracked but did not shatter. He hit it again and this time, glass fell inwards tinkling at the same time.

"Shhhh! hissed Kevin, "You'll wake everyone up makin' that much noise!

Lee ignored Kevin and knocked out more of the glass from the windowpane. He then covered the lip of broken glass that remained on the edge with the material wrapped around his arm and then carefully climbed into the office.

Gorrin stepped outside still in his nightclothes and looked around at the other boats, but could not see anyone lurking in the shadows. He cast his gaze towards the main office and noticed that there was a dark shape moving silently close to the office door. He focused on the figure and noticed that the windowpane was reflecting the street lamp in a strange way.

Gorrin studied the window for a few seconds, before understanding that the person now hiding in the shadows had broken the windowpane. As he continued to observe the shadowy figures, one broke a few more pieces of glass and then placed something over the edge of the window and climbed inside.

Gorrin decided that he was going to intervene – he did not like thieves and was going to make sure that this thief was going to wish that they had not broken into this particular boatyard office. Before moving forward he looked around as he had definitely heard two voices and could not see the second person.

Just then, the second thief appeared from around the side of the office, and moved forward to the front door, while the first thief opened the door into the office. He disappeared inside and Gorrin could then hear a whispered conversation. This was followed by various muffled sounds and the occasional curse as the thieves blundered around in the dark, lit only by the odd flash of a torch as they moved within the office.

Gorrin decided that this was the moment to act. Quickly he muttered the invisibility charm and rubbed the amethyst on the ring. He shimmered, then faded from view. Carefully he crept over to the office and looked inside. As gnomes have very good eyesight, he easily saw the two thieves inside, and he picked up a stone from the ground and threw it at the figure named Lee.

Whack! It struck him straight on the shin. Lee let out a shout and started cursing his fellow thief, asking "What the hell do you think you are doing?"

Kevin, who had been busy rifling various drawers in the office, did not see what had just happened, so he turned and said, "What do you mean?"

Just then another stone rocketed through the doorway to hit Kevin straight in the stomach with such force he doubled up with the blow. "Oof," Kevin exclaimed. Lee had witnessed the stone, fly across his torch beam from the direction of the doorway and was just about to charge outside to deal with their unknown assailant when he was hit on the head by a book from behind. "Ow," said Lee, his head throbbed where the hard back book corner had just caught him on the head.

They both turned to look at this new direction of attack as first, papers, and books, followed quickly by small boxes of boat parts, nuts and bolts cascaded on to them. The noise was now so great, that the lights in the main house had switched on and the sound of police sirens could be heard rapidly approaching.

Gorrin, meanwhile had been having a field day throwing whatever he could lay his hands on at the two thieves. While this was happening the two were now convinced that the place was haunted, as objects just appeared in mid air moments before they were hit by them.

When he thought that the two had been bombarded with enough objects, he pointed his staff at the two and started to chant a sleeping charm. A pink light wafted out of the end of the staff and alighted on the two burglars. They both looked shocked for a few seconds while they were bathed in pink light, seconds later they both crashed to the floor in a deep sleep.

Gorrin smiled and quickly took out a pinch of the faerie dust from the green velvet pouch and threw it into the air, muttering the repair charm. The green sparkling powder glittered in the darkness, then all of the chaos of books, boxes, nuts and bolts flew back to where they had come from and the broken window glass repaired itself.

Once the clean-up was complete, Gorrin again smiled at the sight of the two lying asleep on the office floor. He left the office and crossed the boatyard back to the boat where he watched the police car draw up to meet the boatyard owner. The two policemen and the owner ran over to the office and switched on the light since the door was wide open.

As they looked inside they could not believe what they were seeing, for there in the middle of the office floor were the two thieves. Both were holding money from the till, and both were sound asleep. As quick as the two policemen could, they had placed handcuffs on and arrested them.

Both were well known to the police and were wanted for a string of burglaries and other petty thefts, and so it was with some satisfaction that the two were put into the back of the police car and driven away.

The police car sped away and George the boatyard owner, looked all around at the office, but he could not understand what had just happened. Even more mystifying was the fact that the office actually looked cleaner than it had ever looked. He couldn't fathom out this and was still puzzling this as he locked up the office and went back to his house.

Gorrin had, meanwhile, returned to his cabin. Only then did he remove the invisibility charm as he climbed back into bed where he closed his eyes. He was still smiling as he went to sleep thinking about the events of the night. As he faded into dreamland, he thought that he must remember to write it up tomorrow.

When dawn broke, Gorrin was already up and about. He was dressed and ready for the day as he stepped out on to the deck and looked about. The mist was still present lying over the canal in wispy threads. Gorrin looked about and noticed a couple of geese silently drifting past looking upwards towards Gorrin. They both quacked as if to say 'Good morning' and Gorrin responded by wishing them both a "Good morning" also.

He walked down the boat and under the tarpaulin that served as a makeshift deck cover or tent and headed for Brian's cabin. Outside the door he stopped and listened and smiled as he could clearly hear the sound of Brian snoring. He paused for a few moments and decided to wait a little while before waking Brian. Looking about the boatyard, he became aware of people starting to arrive for their day's work.

Gorrin knocked on Brian's cabin door and let himself in. Brian was still asleep, but he decided that he would try to make a pot of tea – but this time he would be extra careful. Luckily for Gorrin, everything worked properly this time, although he made sure he did not leave the gas running too long, before igniting it. He decided to use his staff to ignite the gas, rather than the matches.

Brian was awoken, by the whistling of the kettle, while Gorrin set about pouring the boiling water into the teapot. Minutes later they were both enjoying an early morning cup of tea. Gorrin quickly related the events of the previous night. Brian sat up in bed looking at Gorrin with an amused grin on his face. He finally remarked to Gorrin. "You know Gorrin, you seem to attract trouble like a magnet and yet you always manage to sort things out. Just how do you manage to do that?"

"I'm lucky I suppose Brian. Well at least in some things, although I do seem to be a bit accident prone in other things," said Gorrin, as he remembered the long sleep and the recent escapade with the gas cooker. Gorrin continued, "In fact I always seemed to have this problem before I went to sleep for three hundred and fifty years, so nothing has changed there."

Gorrin went outside to have a better look around the boatyard, whilst Brian got himself dressed before cooking breakfast for both of them. Of course Gorrin thought it better to be invisible to prevent any awkward questions. Gorrin had come to realise from his conversations with Brian, that gnomes were not a common sight. In fact they were a figure of myth and so he had decided that for the moment until he was better acquainted with the ways of the modern world, he would stay invisible in the towns.

He remembered the time in the past when even then, gnomes were a rare sight and people tended to avoid them as they mistrusted the magic they wielded. As time had moved on, the gnomes had kept themselves more and more to themselves and had tended to avoid dealings with people for much of the time. And people had come to regard gnomes as folklore or fairy tales.

He continued to walk around the boatyard looking at the various boats lying on supports in various stages of maintenance and repair. He had seen boatyards before in his travels before he went for his long sleep, but all the modern cranes and hoists and vehicles in the yard were very different to his recollections of a previous time.

Work had now begun in the boatyard and he watched a man using a tool to drill holes in the side of the boat. On closer inspection, he realised that the man was actually drilling out a strange looking silvery metal lump from the underside of the narrowboat he was working on. The man continued to work on the boat totally unaware that the inquisitive gnome was watching him.

Gorrin walked closer to where the man was working and looked at a box containing a number of the silvery metallic blocks and was very curious. "What were they for?" he wondered, as the man started to fit one to replace the worn out block on the underside of the boat. Gorrin walked around the boat looking up at the underside of the boat and noticed that there were two more of these strange devices fitted on the keel of the boat.

He resolved that he must ask Brian what they were for, as he walked back to the 'Round Tuit'. There was so much of this world he did not understand, he thought. No matter, it was interesting, very interesting indeed. As he re-entered the rear cabin, the smell of frying bacon met him and he instantly felt hungry.

Brian looked up to see Gorrin shimmering into sight. He still had not got used to the way Gorrin shimmered in and out of sight, but he thought he might eventually. Gorrin sat down and ate the bacon sandwich that Brian had prepared him. He sat munching on his sandwich and asked Brian about the silvery lumps of metal.

"They are zinc anodes and are to stop the bottom of the narrowboat from rusting away." Brian explained.

"Well how do they do that?" enquired Gorrin further.

"Well," said Brian, "Science is not my strong point, but as I understand it, they rust instead of the hull, and so every so often you have to take off what is left of the old anodes and replace them with new ones. My boat has got three on it as well."

"I see," said Gorrin. "How interesting?"

Soon breakfast was finished and the plates were washed and put away and Brian announced that he needed to go back to the office. He looked pointedly at Gorrin, then said "No doubt your night activities have got a few people baffled eh?" he chuckled and left the cabin.

While Brian was sorting out the boat cargo, Gorrin decided that he would explore the boatyard a little more thoroughly, but again invisible. So he quickly shimmered from view and went outside to have a look around. As he wandered around the yard, he noticed that the driver of one of the cranes was now moving the crane into a position to lift a recently arrived narrowboat out of the canal. Slings had been fitted to the underside of the boat and the crane was slowly lifting the boat out of the water.

The boat gradually left the canal as it was hoisted into the air and water cascaded in rivulets, to fall into the canal and splash on to the wharf. Slowly Will, the crane driver, manoeuvred the boat around into a position ready to lower on to the boat chocks. Just as the boat was starting to lower, the narrowboat shifted in the slings and the whole thing started to tilt in a crazy fashion.

Gorrin, who had been watching this, realised that something was wrong and that the boat was about to slip out of the sling and come crashing to the ground. He rapidly raised his staff that he had been holding and started to softly sing a charm. The runes on the staff, glowed purple and a purple light shot out of the end of the staff to strike the boat and sling. Instantly the boat stopped slipping and the crane operator quickly lowered the boat.

The crane driver stared at the strange purple beam that seemed to originate out of thin air to strike the side of the boat sling. He had no idea what was causing it, only that it seemed to be stopping a nasty accident from happening.

At the same time that this was happening, Brian had just left the office and was now observing the events as they unfolded, along with everyone else in the boatyard. The boat reached the wooden chocks and as soon as that occurred, the purple light winked out of existence. The crane driver climbed out of the cab and ran over to the boat to check on any damage, but of course, there was none. Bewildered the driver scratched his head and frowned, then shrugged his shoulders and started to unhook the slings from the boat.

Gorrin had decided at this point that he had better not make his presence known quite so obviously and so he returned to the boat. He sat on one of the mooring bollards and looked over to where Brian was approaching. He noticed that Brian was frowning. "I wonder what the matter is?" thought Gorrin.

~~~~~~~~~~~~~~~~

Chapter Eight
"The Coin Collector"

Brian called out softly to where he thought Gorrin was standing, but of course as he couldn't see him it was only a guess.

"I am over here," said Gorrin. "Sitting on the bollard. Anyway, what's the matter Brian? You look little unhappy."

Brian paused for a few seconds before replying, and then said, "It's the council; they have changed their minds about where they want the stone delivered to."

Gorrin digested this information before replying, then said; "Well where do they want it delivered to then?"

"Only down the River Avon, that all!" Brian retorted sarcastically, then quickly apologised as it really wasn't Gorrin's fault at all, but he felt he needed to take his frustration out on someone and poor Gorrin was the only one around.

"Sorry Gorrin, that outburst was uncalled for. It's not your fault, it's the ruddy council; they never seem to be able to make up their minds and then stick to it. Oh well." finished Brian.

"Well, at least I will get to have a trip down the river." Gorrin paused then added hopefully, "If that's alright with you Brian?"

"It's no problem Gorrin, I will be more than happy, but please try to limit your use of magic as it's beginning to attract attention and someone might put two and two together and link the strange happenings with my boat," Brian replied.

It was now Gorrin's turn to apologise, "Sorry Brian, but I couldn't let those thieves get away with it could I? And if I hadn't intervened when that boat slipped, there could have been a very nasty accident. "

"I suppose so", said Brian. "Anyway, good work on stopping those two thieves. I gather from speaking to the boat owner, that the police have been questioning them and they keep saying this place is haunted. I had a job to keep a straight face when George, the owner told me. That wasn't a problem Gorrin, but the purple light appearing in the middle of the yard when the boat started to slip did look a little peculiar to say the least."

"Mm, I didn't think at the time, I just sort of acted." Gorrin said. "Anyway, you didn't say where we have got to go to with the boat to unload the stone."

"Well, they now want me to unload only half of this cargo here and then take the rest of it down to Evesham now. Originally I was to deliver it to this boatyard and take a cargo back up to Market Drayton but some bright spark has done a deal with another council and now they want me take half of this one down to Evesham marina. I wish I could get my hands on the 'Charlie' that arranged this. I'd give him a piece of my mind, make no mistake."

Brian continued along this line for a little while longer then, stopped and looked in the direction of where he thought Gorrin was sitting and said, "Sorry for going on a bit, but I needed to let off steam."

Gorrin tactfully responded, "Oh don't worry Brian, I could see you were a little peeved to say the least, so I just let you carry on until you had finished. I'm sure I would feel the same, were I in your shoes. Look on the bright side; at least you will have the 'pleasure' of my company for a little longer at least!" Then Gorrin chuckled.

Brian countered: "Gorrin, I value your company and you are no trouble at all." Then he looked sideways towards Gorrin's voice and added, "But unless you can stand there visible, they are going to think I am off my rocker talking to thin air! Now then," he continued, "you are very sensible most of the time, but I think we need to get you some more modern clothes, then you won't stand out quite so much, and then you can become visible."

Gorrin raised a slightly singed eyebrow and then replied, "That sounds an interesting idea, but where do I get money from to buy my clothes with. I'm sure my money is out of date and I won't be able to spend it."

Brian looked interested immediately and said, "Come back into the boat and we will have a look at your money, it might be worth more than you think Gorrin."

Brian climbed back on to the canal boat and was followed almost immediately by Gorrin and as he entered the cabin, he shimmered into view. Thrusting his hand into one of his tunic pockets he pulled out a leather pouch tied with a leather thong. He removed the thong and poured the contents on to the little cabin table.

Brian stared transfixed by the gold and silver coins that were spilling on to the table, and as one of the coins rolled across and looked as though it was going to roll off the table completely, he grabbed the coin and held it up to the light. Sure enough, it was made of gold and was Roman in origin. He put it down and looked at the others, there were silver, gold and bronze coins of many different types – a veritable treasure trove to collectors he thought.

"Gorrin," Brian announced. "Those coins are worth a lot of money to a collector. We should be able to easily sell them through a jewellers or antique collectors shop. But if we try to sell them all at once they might start asking awkward questions and we don't want to get drawn into that do we, eh?"

Gorrin thought for a moment then answered, "Alright Brian, if you are sure, you pick a few good ones and I'll put the rest away."

Brian pondered himself for a few more seconds before replying, "Look, it's only a guess as I am no coin expert, but I reckon that one and that one will do for a start," he pointed to the two Roman coins, then added; "And that one and that one." Two more coins, but silver this time, were selected. Gorrin scooped up the rest into the leather pouch and put it back into his tunic.

"Once we have got the coins exchanged for cash we can then set about buying you some new clothes eh?" said Brian.

"OK," said Gorrin. This was a new expression for Gorrin, but he liked the singsong way you could say it.

Gorrin asked another question before they left. "What about unloading the cargo Brian?"

"Oh, don't worry about that Gorrin, they'll do that, and they will load the new cargo," said Brian.

And so the two left the boat and stepped on to the canal towpath, with Gorrin carrying his magic backpack. To anyone looking, it looked comical, Gorrin was dressed in his red tunic, red trousers, black boots, and his red hat. Brian was dressed in jeans and a woollen sweater, with an armless jacket pulled over the top. As they walked out of the boatyard and on to the canal towpath, a couple of the boat maintenance personnel gazed at them briefly, before resuming their repair work.

George, the boatyard owner, who did not miss a trick normally, when it came down to operations within his yard, spotted them as they left and stared after them until they disappeared around the corner out of sight. He looked thoughtfully into space for a few moments, then smiled a secret smile, raised an eyebrow and then resumed his paperwork.

They continued along the towpath, past a number of bridges until they reached a point where the towpath disappeared as it passed through an inaccessible corridor towards the river Avon. At this point they had to leave the path and they crossed via a bridge and headed on into the town along a road.

As they walked along the road together, a couple of teenagers who were walking in the opposite direction on the other side of the road, cat-called, shouting, "Hey you, bit early for fancy dress aren't you?" This was followed with, "Hey, missing your fishing rod ain't ya." The comments continued but Brian and Gorrin ignored them, although Brian was getting angry on Gorrin's behalf.

Gorrin didn't understand all the inferences in the taunts, but he understood enough to know that they were insults, rather than compliments. He looked up at Brian, as he could see that he was doing his best to keep his anger under control. Gorrin realised that his friend was still annoyed with the way he had been treated by the council and this new verbal attack was just something else to antagonise him.

Gorrin spoke to Brian, "Brian, don't worry about it, I'm not bothered, it's their problem not mine."

Brian looked down at him and replied, "Yes, but it doesn't make it right though does it?"

As they continued along the road, Brian spoke again, "I think that you had better remove the hat – I think it's the hat that is making you look a little unusual."

Gorrin nodded and took the hat off and pushed it into one of his deep tunic pockets. They continued to walk in silence as they approached the outer area of the town of Stratford-upon-Avon, Gorrin looking all about at the many changes that had occurred. A number of cars swept past and as they did so the wind of their passage ruffled Gorrin's hair and beard. He noticed the strange smell from these vehicles that was the same as the smell of the boat engine fumes and of course the bulldozer that had awoken him, all those days ago.

Eventually they reached the town itself and as it was not even nine in the morning, the traffic was just beginning to get busy. They waited for the traffic to pass then crossed the road. They passed a number of shops and Gorrin suddenly noticed that one of the shops had a number of baskets on the pavement outside the shop. There were various different items in the baskets, from clothes pegs to small garden tools, but then Gorrin noticed a number of small figures.

Gorrin stopped in his tracks and stared at the figurines before picking one up. His astonishment turned to a scowl as he realised that these figures were none other than gnomes! Or, at least, that was what they were supposed to resemble. He dropped the figure he was holding and picked a box up that contained another of the figures. He studied the picture on the side of the box. This was one that was supposed to be fishing beside an ornamental pond.

Brian had meanwhile, continued along the pavement and had not noticed that Gorrin was no longer walking beside. That was, until Brian spoke to him, and after a few seconds pause, he looked down to see why Gorrin had not answered. He stopped dead in his tracks and looked around quickly to see where the little gnome could have gone. As he scanned back along the road, he spotted Gorrin holding a small box.

He quickly retraced his steps back to his friend looking closely at the gnome as he did so. As Brian drew closer, he understood the reason for the scowl on Gorrin's face - the detail on the box the gnome was holding clearly showed a bright yellow character of a painted gnome.

'Oops', thought Brian, 'Maybe I should have told him about such things. Well it's too late now; I just hope he doesn't react badly.'

For a few more moments, Gorrin continued to scowl, then his right eyebrow raised itself slightly and he gripped his runic staff tightly. Gorrin's face gradually changed as the first signs of a laugh made its appearance. His hand on the staff relaxed and he let out a great burst of laughter.

"Well, I never seen anything so ridiculous in my life," said Gorrin, then he added, "And now I know what those lads were on about," The laughter spread to Brian, though in Brian's case it was more relief that Gorrin had not decided to use his staff to blow the figures up, or worse!

A few passers-by looked at the scene as they passed, one of them saying "A bit early for trick or treat aren't we?"

Brian turned to the man who had made the comment and said, "You don't know the half mate, you really don't."

Gorrin recovered his composure and asked Brian a question, "OK Brian, what is this all about then?"

Brian replied, "Well Gorrin, those are garden ornaments and are put in peoples gardens to provide a little charm."

"Well," responded Gorrin, "I find that really quite ironic, considering that in the past us gnomes have been shunned, to such an extent that we are only regarded as folklore and myth. I think the joke is on you humans and not gnomes."

Brian, thought about this for a few seconds and then replied, "You are quite right Gorrin, in fact before I met you, I only every considered gnomes to be fairy stories and not actual fact. It just shows how wrong one can be."

Gorrin put the small cardboard box down back into the basket and turned back to Brian, saying, "Come on then Brian, let's find this collectors shop, or whatever it is we are going to look for." And with that both continued on along the pavement further into the town. As they wandered along, Gorrin kept looking in all of the shops and tried to ignore the few curious stares that they were greeted with.

Eventually, they found the shop they were looking for. They heard a little bell ring as they entered and then ring again as the door closed. They both walked over to the shop counter that was made of glass and contained within the counter were various coins of many different types. Gorrin gazed into the brightly lit interior of the glass cabinet and studied the coins.

Brian was about to call out for assistance, when they heard movement from a doorway behind the counter and a small elderly man appeared. He said, "Good morning Sir, How can I help you?"

The shop owner, was wearing a brightly coloured bow tie and a checked waistcoat. On top of his greying receding hair were perched a small pair of round glasses. Small brown eyes peered at Brian.

Brian deposited the coins from out of his pocket on to the velvet material that lay on the top of the glass counter, saying, "I would like to sell these coins please."

Francis, the shop owner looked down at the coins, then back at Brian. He paused then said pointedly "I take that these are yours?"

"Well actually," replied Brian, "They are his." He nodded in the direction of Gorrin who had been crouching down still looking at the coins inside the brightly lit glass counter. At this moment Gorrin stood up, but since he was only three foot six inches high in his black boots, this did not make a very imposing sight.

"His?" queried Francis.

"Yes, mine," said Gorrin. "And they have been in my family a long time." As he said this, his eyebrow went up and a slight smile played at the edges of his mouth.

"Okay," said Francis slowly, "I have to ask, you know. I have good reputation and I don't want to ruin it by getting involved with any property of questionable origin."

"Are you implying that this is stolen?" said Brian, raising his voice slightly. "Well it isn't, and as my friend has just said, it has been in his family a long time." Brian had caught the humour in what Gorrin had meant and decided to continue in the same vein himself.

"Okay, okay, I didn't mean to imply anything, but you cannot be too careful these days," said Francis. He picked up a coin and drew a small magnifying tube from the pocket in his waistcoat. He put the tube up to his eye and studied the coin for a few moments.

As he studied the gold coin, it sparkled where it caught the daylight. He carefully put the coin down and picked up the others in turn and studied them one by one. Eventually he had completed the inspection; he looked up at the two who were waiting patiently, before he spoke.

"Do you know how much these are worth? They are prime specimens and are very valuable. Do you have any more of them?"

Gorrin replied, "Yes, but I want to keep them for the moment."

"Oh!" replied Francis, "Are you sure?" he persisted.

"Yes, quite sure," said Gorrin.

"Okay, then," the shop owner paused as he re-examined the coins, "I'll give you, well I'll give you five hundred a piece for the gold ones and two hundred and one hundred for the others, making a grand total of thirteen hundred pounds."

"I think that is cheap and you will now give us a better offer," said Brian forcefully. He stared intently at the shop owner and the shop owner looked back across at Brian. The shop owner's eyes narrowed. He paused slightly before he continued; "I can see you are a shrewd business man, so I will not mess you around. All right, six hundred and fifty each for the two gold ones, and three hundred and two hundred for the other two. That's my best and final offer."

Gorrin looked at Brian and then nodded, "Done!" said Gorrin. "I'll accept that price."

The man looked back at Gorrin and then at Brian, and went over to the till and asked; "Will you take a cheque?"

"No, the cash please, oh and don't say you don't carry that sort of money, because I know you do, otherwise we would not have come here," Brian replied.

"Cash it is then," said Francis, and with that he opened the till and took out the correct amount of money and placed it on to the black velvet on the counter.

Brian picked the money up counted it and gave it to Gorrin, who politely thanked both Brian and the shop owner. As they turned to leave the shop, the owner of the shop spoke; "Look, anytime you are passing and feel that you want to do some more business, then, please feel free. Good day to you both," and with that he inclined his head in a half-nod.

Brian and Gorrin both nodded as they left the shop, the bell jingling again as the door closed. Once back out in the street they both grinned at each other and walked on down the street to the main shopping area on the high street.

~~~~~~~~~~~~~~~~~~~~~~

Several minutes had passed by this time and Gorrin was still debating with Brian, as to whether to use magic. While they were debating this, the main light in the lift failed and the emergency back-up blinked on, but only for a few seconds before it too failed and Brian and Gorrin were plunged into darkness. All they could see from within the lift was a chink of light just creeping through the join in the outer doors, but this was insufficient to provide any meaningful illumination.

As they stood there in the near darkness, Gorrin's nose wrinkled. What was that funny smell? It reminded him of the same sort of pungent sharp odour that you got after a severe thunderstorm, except there was another strange smell mixed with it. Brian could now also smell the sharp odour and he recognised the smell of burning plastic insulation and electrics almost immediately. Equally, he recognised that they needed to get out of the lift as soon as possible as there might be a fire starting. He told Gorrin just what he thought was happening.

Gorrin acted immediately. He tapped his staff three times on the floor of the lift and uttered a phrase from an ancient language and immediately runes on the staff glowed blue white. The head of the walking staff then lit up into a blue white light that illuminated the inside of the lift. Gorrin looked across at Brian, who nodded his thanks back. At least they could now see what they were doing now, thought Brian.

Chapter Nine
"Books & New Clothes for Gorrin"

Walking down the high street, Gorrin was busily looking in all the various shop windows and was fascinated at the range of products. One shop particularly caught Gorrin's eye – it was a bookshop, with a large numbers of books displayed, on topics that he had never dreamt of. Indeed, the sheer numbers and the colour photographs were a complete surprise.

Gorrin kept asking more and more questions and as Brian explained about photographs, the little gnome spotted a book on food. On the front cover was a picture of a large casserole with mushrooms in a nice rich sauce. Gorrin's mouth watered at the thought and he gazed longingly at the picture, while he listed to Brian.

"I would like to buy that book," said Gorrin, pointing at the one that had caught his interest, "I think that it would make a nice addition to my library at home."

Brian looked at the book that Gorrin was pointing at and said, "What, that one on ' Casseroles and Stews?"

"Yes, that's the one," said Gorrin. "I like the look of that mushroom casserole."

"Okay," said Brian, and with that they both headed back to the doorway and entered the shop.

On entering the shop, Gorrin's eyes were everywhere. He had never been in a bookshop before that had so many books on sale. He picked up the first one he could and opened the pages and looked inside. Peering back at him were people wearing all types of clothing. The particular book that he just happened to have picked up was concerned with costume through the ages, from the Ice Age to the present. Although the pictures were all drawings rather than photographs, they were all beautifully drawn. He flicked through the book, marvelling at the neatness of the printing. When he had last looked at books, although they were printed on a press, they were very expensive, with very few copies around. He stopped, when he came to the picture showing the types of clothing that people had been wearing when he went into hibernation, following the mistake with the charm.

He continued on through the book until he reached the present day, completely fascinated by the pictures. Brian had meanwhile, found the book that Gorrin had wanted and had walked back to where his friend was still standing.

"Here you are Gorrin, I've found the book you wanted. Come on, we'll go and pay for it."

"I'll have this one as well Brian," said Gorrin. "It looks very interesting and perhaps it'll help me catch up with what has happened over the years."

Brian looked thoughtful at this point and replied, "Well Gorrin, I think we could find a better book, if its history you want to read about."

"Well, I still want this book as I like the pictures, but we can still look for the history book as well." Gorrin said.

And so they spent the next hour wandering around the bookshop, while a few curious shoppers looked at Gorrin and smiled or looked puzzled, depending on their demeanour. Finally, they found what they wanted – a short history of Britain, from the Middle Ages to the present. They wandered over to the till and the young shop assistant looked down at Gorrin and then up at Brian. The pile of books that they had collected in the blue plastic basket, they now deposited on the counter surface. The books were scanned by the assistant on the till and as the prices appeared on the electronic display, Gorrin looked on fascinated at the bright green flickering numbers on the till.

"Twenty-five pounds please?" requested the shop assistant.

With a look of astonishment on his face, Gorrin said "How much?"

His voice went up as he said this, then he continued, "Prices have gone up." Tucking his staff through his belt, he took his leather pouch out of his tunic pocket and opened it and pulled out a large number of twenty-pound and ten-pound notes. Gorrin stared at them, and gave thirty pounds to the girl. The till opened and the correct change was handed back to Gorrin.

Once the books were safely into the plastic carrier bag, Gorrin opened his backpack and placed the bag inside it. There was a slight sparkle as Gorrin withdrew his hands and the bag shimmered and disappeared. Brian had been looking down at Gorrin as this occurred and had seen the books shimmer and disappear. He raised his eyes quickly to see if the shop assistant had witnessed this little display of real magic, but the girl had been occupied with her nails and had missed the event.

Phew, thought Brian, that could have been a bit awkward to explain. And with that, Gorrin fastened the bag and put it back on his back and then removed the walking staff from his belt. Together they left the shop and continued on along the high street.

Brian suggested that they look for a department store where they should be able to buy suitable clothes and since Gorrin had no idea as to what a department store was, he agreed. Shortly they came to the store that Brian had in mind and they walked up the steps into the large shop. If Gorrin was curious before, then his curiosity was whetted even more by the multitude of goods on sale within this shop.

Brian watched Gorrin as he looked around at the many different clothes arranged in racks and stands. "Er Gorrin," said Brian, "Those are ladies clothes!" I think we will need the children's department don't you think?"

Gorrin became a little indignant at this, until he caught sight of the grin on Brian's face and realised that his friend was having a little joke at his expense. As soon as Gorrin recognised that this was a joke, his face cracked into a grin and he smiled.

"Yes okay Brian, but I want to have a look at the men's clothes as well. I was only trying to compare what is on the stand to what I saw in the book."

This conversation had drawn a few quizzical looks from the various shop assistants, as the brightly coloured gnome was not something that one saw every day!

"Come on then," said Brian, "We'll use the escalator."

"What's an escalator?" asked Gorrin. Brian explained that it was a sort of moving staircase.

"That sounds like fun," exclaimed Gorrin. Once they had stepped on to the escalator, Gorrin looked around as they slowly rose up to the next floor and saw that the store seemed to stretch in all directions for some considerable distance. In all his long life, he had never ever been inside such a large shop and was more than a little surprised at the sheer size of it.

They both stepped off at the end of the ride and Brian steered Gorrin over to the children's clothing. As they wandered along looking at the clothes, Gorrin's expression varied from a frown to simply wrinkling up his nose as he looked at some of the fashions that he certainly did not like. Eventually Brian pointed to a rack of dark green cargo pants that seemed to have a multitude of pockets. He really quite liked them, as they were a colour he liked and had many useful pockets.

He picked out a second pair in a dark maroon colour, that he also liked then moved on to the area where the shirts were displayed. There were shirts of all types and colours and Gorrin had a hard task trying to limit the numbers he wanted to pick, but he finally settled on seven shirts that were long sleeved.

Placing the shirts in the basket that his friend was carrying, Brian directed Gorrin towards the changing rooms so that Gorrin could try on the new clothes. Taking the basket with him into the small changing room area, Gorrin disappeared behind a curtain, while Brian sat down outside to await the reappearance of the gnome.

A few minutes went by and Brian was just beginning to get concerned when Gorrin reappeared wearing the dark green cargo pants and dark green shirt. "I like these the best," said Gorrin, "Though the others are quite smart as well."

Brian nodded his approval and Gorrin said that he wanted to keep them on, but Brian had to explain that he would have to pay for them first. Gorrin reluctantly returned to the cubicle to change and returned a few moments later in his original clothing.

"You will need a good coat for when it gets cold and wet, Gorrin."

Gorrin agreed and they headed for a different part of the department store, picking up a couple of thick woollen jumpers along the way. They reached the outdoor clothing section and Gorrin decided that he was going to try on every coat he could, much to the amusement of Brian.

The gnome was now spoilt for choice as he could not make up his mind, and for many minutes he mulled over the different coats. He finally picked two and placed them over his arm. Brian was quite loaded up with all the different articles of clothing as they now headed for one of the tills.

"Oh I nearly forgot," said Brian, "You will need a hat". Stopping to pick up a black and white woollen hat in a Lapland style, with reindeer decorating it, Gorrin placed this on to his head and they continued walking to the checkout.

Very soon the goods were totalled and the bill paid by Gorrin – again he was surprised by the (to him) high cost of clothes. Gorrin had to keep reminding himself that such a long time had passed, that prices had changed a lot in the intervening years.

With all the purchases now safely enclosed in the store bags, they were on their way out, when an old lady in one of the adjacent aisles slipped and gashed her leg and she sat down on the floor with a thump. One of the shop assistants had witnessed this accident and rushed over to assist. The assistant looked briefly at the nasty cut and bruise that was swiftly forming on her shin. She panicked and blurted out that she was not to worry as she was going to get help.

Gorrin had also seen the accident and he quickly thought of a suitable plan to help. Quickly rushing over to the old lady, he took off his pack and opened it, calling for the healing salve. The jar of healing liniment shimmered into view inside the pack, sparkling with stars and Gorrin promptly removed the jar and opened it, using a finger he dipped it into the translucent gel and applied the gel to the nasty cut on her leg.

The old lady was too shocked to protest and simply looked on stunned as the blood started to seep through her tights and run down her leg. As Gorrin applied the gel to the wound, something strange then happened to the cut. As soon as the gel was applied, the gel seemed to flow around the wound then disappear, taking with it any evidence that there had ever been a bruise or cut on the leg. Gorrin stood up and smiled down at the old lady and offered his hand.

For a few seconds the lady just stared down at the now rapidly disappearing bruise and then back at Gorrin. She reached out with her hand and the little gnome pulled her to her feet. She was amazed at the apparent strength in this short bearded man and she smiled back as she realised that any injury that she might have had did not now seem to exist.

"Thank-you young man!" she said and Gorrin beamed back, then he gave a little bow and walked away with Brian, heading in the direction of the lift this time. Gorrin chuckled at this and then walked away leaving the bemused woman looking at his retreating figure.

Brian looked down at Gorrin as they walked away and said, "That was a good thing you did there my old friend, though I had to smile when she said, "*Young man!*"

"So did I my friend, so did I," said Gorrin.

"I think she is going to have a hard time explaining how the leg was mended though." Brian added.

They reached the lifts and Gorrin looked on curiously. "What are these lifts?"

"Well," said Brian, "They move you up and down between floors quickly. They are useful if you are carrying a lot of shopping," he said looking at Gorrin pointedly, "Or if you cannot walk up the stairs or use the escalator. The Americans called them elevators."

"I see," said Gorrin.

Just then one of the lifts opened its doors and a strangely tinny female voice said "First floor- children's clothes and haberdashery." Gorrin looked in, but could see no one. He looked up at Brian and said "Magic? Or is someone throwing their voice?"

"No Gorrin, that is an automatic voice system, it comes from that grill in the side of the lift." Brian explained.

"That's clever," said Gorrin. "Well you might not be able to do magic in this century, but you have managed to do lots of other things."

They stepped into the lift and Brian pressed the button marked '*Ground*' and they waited whilst the voice announced, "Doors closing, mind the doors please!" whereupon, the two lift doors closed and lift started to move upward.

"I thought we were supposed to be going down in this lift and not up," Gorrin stated.

"We were," said Brian, "But I think someone on the top floor has pressed a button before we did, so now it's heading up there first."

Gorrin raised both his eyebrows at this, and Brian just nodded in return. The lift gradually rose higher and higher, up though the building until it reached the top floor and the lift finally stopped.

However, the doors did not open and the lift did not move. Brian looked at Gorrin and Gorrin looked back at Brian. "I thought these doors were supposed to open Brian," Gorrin exclaimed.

"They seem to have stuck Gorrin," said Brian, "We will have to press the alarm button."

Meanwhile outside, a woman wearing a smart trouser suit was becoming more and more impatient with every passing second and was now repeatedly pressing the lift call button, but of course to no avail. She scowled at the button and then at the doors and let out a "Harrumph" sound and walked away in a decided huff, leaving the two still in the lift.

Back inside the lift, Gorrin was debating with Brian what they should do. Gorrin was all for using magic to solve the problem, but Brian was concerned that a more blatant use of magic in such a public way would attract far too much attention. Gorrin on the other hand, kept saying that he would use the repair magic dust and it shouldn't cause any side effects, hopefully, but of course, he could not guarantee that would actually be the case.

The debate continued, but in the meantime, others in the store had tried to use the lift and had been unable to get any response from the system. It became apparent, to one of the store floor managers, that there was a problem with the lift system, as now all of the lifts were not working and the lights on the instrument panel had now decided to fail.

Quickly, the floor manager radioed the main office, using his store walkie-talkie and the office in turn, called out the town's fire brigade, as this was a potential emergency since it was believed that there were two people within the lift.

Outside the store, the fire brigade had now arrived and were busy collecting all the equipment necessary for them to achieve a rescue of 'persons reported' within a lift. The crew quickly entered the building and were met by the store manager who accompanied them to the lifts. Briefly outlining what had apparently happened, he directed the two fire officers towards a nearby stairwell.

The two officers headed for the lift plant room at the top of the stairwell, while the crew at the fire appliance radioed a situation report back to the command and control centre. On reaching the plant room, they felt the door surface. It was not very hot but was quite warm. Carefully the senior officer opened the door with a master key, pushing the door open and standing to one side, just in case there was a flashover.

There was no flash, but the air within the room was very warm with a strong acrid electrical odour mixed with burning rubber and plastic. Wisps of smoke eddied out into the stairwell. As they looked into the room, they spotted a small electrical fire next to the main control panel. Armed with a dry powder extinguisher, they put the fire out and isolated the electrical panel using the main master power breaker. That action completed, they radioed their status to the fire engine and awaited the arrival of the lift maintenance, whom they had been told were due to arrive within the next few minutes.

Gorrin and Brian knew nothing of these events trapped as they were within the lift and Brian had finally agreed that they needed to do something quickly to try to get out of the lift as a fire appeared to be underway. Gorrin had decided by this point that he was going to use the teleportation powder. This was likely to be dangerous, as he could not clearly see where they were going to teleport to. It was quite possible that if he made a mistake, they could wind up inside a brick wall or a floor.

Gorrin explained to Brian, the potential risks of this course of action, but Brian was convinced that they needed to get out of the lift as soon as possible as he had no intention of being cooked inside a steel box, like an oven ready chicken!

Gorrin took out the purple velvet pouch from one of his tunic pockets and threw a pinch of the powder over himself and Brian. He uttered a song and for a split second, nothing seemed to happen, then there was a 'pop' and they both disappeared out of the lift.

To Brian, one second they were inside the lift, with the inside lit up by the blue-white light from the staff, and the next the surroundings just faded away to whiteness, then just as suddenly they reappeared outside the lift, amongst a boxed display of electrical appliances. The pyramid of boxes collapsed with a clatter as the two materialised among the display. A small child, who had wandered off from its mother, gaped for a few seconds, before running off shouting that a funny little man had just appeared out of thin air and knocked a load of boxes down.

Hastily, Brian and Gorrin left the mayhem they had just wrought on the stand and walked as quickly as possible away. They left the store and passed the fire officers, who had just managed to open the lift door with the aid of a special key and mechanical handle. The floor manager was astonished when they opened the doors to find that there was nobody inside the lift. He was positive that there had been two people within the lift and as Gorrin and Brian walked past, he recognised them.

Gorrin smiled politely at the man in the suit near the lift as they walked past and the floor manager could not believe his eyes. All he could say was "How, but, how?" of course, by this time Gorrin and Brian were now almost out of the store. Brian remarked to Gorrin as they left, "He's going to have a hard time explaining that to his boss!"

~~~~~~~~~~~~~~~~~~~~~

Chapter Ten
"Televisions and Contracts"

Walking through the town, Gorrin's eyes were roving everywhere. So much had changed since he was last in Stratford; however, he noticed that some of the buildings were original, but one of the largest changes he noticed, was the smell, or rather, the lack of it. Towns and cities were considerably smellier in the 1650s than they now were; in fact disease was rife in some of the places he had visited back then. He thought about this for a moment recalling how a certain gnome who had gone 'bad' had used to cause all sorts of mischief in those days. He shuddered at the thought and dismissed it from his mind.

As they passed the brightly lit shop window jam-packed with all types of silvery looking boxes, Gorrin noticed moving images. He stopped in his tracks to have a closer look and peering through the glass studied the fairy that appeared to be dancing on a tree branch. As the fairy danced, the colours of its wings shimmered with a kaleidoscope of different colours.

Brian had noticed that his companion had stopped to look in the shop window and he walked back to see what Gorrin was looking at. On seeing the picture moving on the computer screen he explained that it was a computer and that the picture was a 'screen-saver'

Of course, Gorrin's immediate response was, "What's a computer and what is a screen-saver?" Brian then spent the next couple of minutes trying to explain. Eventually, Gorrin thought he understood and asked if they could go into the shop and have a look around.

Once inside the shop, Gorrin moved around looking at the different computers until he espied the televisions at the rear of the shop. His eyes lit up as he saw the large moving coloured images and he made a beeline straight for this section. Gnomes can move very quickly when they want to and the speed of his movement attracted the attention of one of the shop assistants.

Keith was responsible for the audio-visual section in the store and was very good at his job. His sales turnover was second to none and he prided himself on running a well-organised section. The rapid arrival of a child, dressed in what appeared to be a garden gnome costume had attracted his attention. He intended to eject this potential troublemaker at the first hint of a problem, so he intercepted the figure in green.

"Do you need any help er...sir?" asked the assistant, who had just realised that this figure in green who looked like he had just come from a fancy dress party, was not a child but a small man with greying hair and a grey short pointed beard and was carrying an elaborately decorated walking stick. As he looked at the little man, he was struck by the way his blue eyes seemed to twinkle.

"What are these? Gorrin asked almost immediately, to the shop assistant. At that moment, Brian who had seen his friend suddenly head off to the far side of the shop had quickly followed.

"Those are televisions Gorrin?" said Brian, a little breathlessly.

At this statement, the shop assistant had looked up at this newcomer. The assistants face showed surprise at the comment Brian had made, as it implied that the small man in the green suit and black boots had never seen a television before.

"Er yes," said the assistant, "They come in a range of sizes." To give the assistant his due, he had recovered his composure very rapidly and was quickly getting his mind into sales mode, now he understood that this was a 'real' potential customer.

"And prices no doubt" added Brian quickly.

Distracted by the brightly-coloured fast moving images, on one of the large flatscreen televisions, a scene had just caught Gorrin's attention. Large numbers of soldiers were trying to land on a beach and other soldiers were firing guns at them. With explosions flying across the screen, Gorrin stood astonished at what was happening – he had only ever seen fighting from a distance and had always made it a point to stay away from such trouble.

In fact, it was part of *The Gnome Code* to try to keep out of major human affairs. Gorrin looked up at Brian and he looked back at Gorrin and the screen. He recognised the scene and said to Gorrin; "That is not happening now, Gorrin. That is a film showing the D-Day landings. They took place about sixty years ago. Oh, and that is a film, not the real thing. It is called entertainment."

Gorrin fell silent for a few seconds, before commenting: "It seems you humans have not gotten over your liking for war then?"

Brian was a little surprised at this directness and considered his reply before he answered.

"No," said Brian, "And we still seem to keep making the same mistakes."

The assistant who had overheard this conversation, was quite perplexed by the discussion that was now ensuing. He spoke up, to try to bring the subject back to the televisions in the sale.

Gorrin, looked back at the assistant, who was rapidly running through the specifications of the different models, then back at the different pictures on the screens. On one of the screens, a new programme was in progress and it caught Gorrin's attention. Brian looked at what Gorrin was watching and quickly realised that the programme was one of the *24 Hour News* channels.

The programme fascinated Gorrin as it moved through the different topics, and then suddenly Gorrin turned round to Brian and asked him a question. Brian was half prepared by the query, since, as soon as they had entered the shop, he half guessed that Gorrin would ask him it. "Brian, why haven't you got a Television?" The gnome enquired.

Brian had made a conscious decision when he embarked on his lifestyle change to become somewhat minimalist. And that meant not using a television, as he believed that most of the news reported these days was bad anyway. Brian thought for a moment before replying.

"Well Gorrin, I used to have one, but I decided I could do without one – I would rather read than watch television."

"I see," said Gorrin, "but you will miss all the news in the world."

"Exactly my point," said Brian.

Again the sales assistant tried to intervene to make a sale, but he stopped short when Brian looked sharply at him.

"Well, do they have small ones that you can travel with?" asked Gorrin, "I think it would be a good way to keep up to date with the news."

Keith, the sales assistant quickly answered: "Yes sir, we have several models that you can take with you."

"Except you don't have a TV licence Gorrin," said Brian.

"What is a TV licence Brian," Gorrin queried.

"You cannot operate a TV without one Gorrin, otherwise you can end up being fined a lot of money," Brian replied.

At this point Gorrin looked dismayed by the news that a TV licence would be needed in order to be able to use a television. "Well that's no good, are you sure?" persisted Gorrin. This time it was the sales assistant's turn to speak up, "Yes sir, it's the law, you cannot operate a TV without a licence. You can of course buy one from the Post Office."

"That's all right if you have a fixed abode," said Brian.

"What do you mean, Brian?" Gorrin enquired once more.

"It means somewhere that you live, and in your case, that might be a little difficult…if you take my meaning," Brian elaborated.

At this point Gorrin understood where Brian was going with the conversation. He could hardly say he lived underground in tunnels within a wooded copse, away from where most people would call a home. Gorrin thought for a few seconds longer and then spoke, "You are right Brian, and I can hardly say where I live, can I?"

The assistant had by this time concluded that the small man wasn't going to buy a television after all, so he turned his attention to Brian. "Well, what about you sir? Surely you would consider one of our latest portable sets?"

"No thank-you, I am fine without such things. I haven't got one now and I certainly don't want one at the moment. "

And so after much debate the two left the shop, while the shop assistant could only shake his head and say to no one in particular, "What a couple of oddballs. In fact the small guy must have been living on another planet. Now there's a thought!" Another prospective customer had just entered the shop and so Keith put all thoughts of this strange encounter out of his mind and started to ask this new customer if he needed any help.

Out on the street again, they started back to the boat in earnest. Before returning to the boatyard, Brian said that they needed to collect some food essentials from a food shop. Brian, mindful of the time and effort that it had taken within the electronics store suggested that perhaps Gorrin could wait outside while Brian went in and got the items they needed.

While Brian went inside, Gorrin lingered outside looking in through the shop window at all the various products on sale.

He sat outside on a bollard while he waited and it wasn't long before Brian reappeared with a couple of plastic carrier bags full of groceries. Gorrin looked at them with interest, but decided not to ask Brian what he had bought as Brian had a look on his face that shouted, *please don't ask me what I have bought.*

Soon they were back on the towpath and could see the boatyard and Brian's boat moored there. Drawing closer, Brian could see that the cargo the council had wanted unloading, had been and was now neatly stacked near to the edge of the boatyard apron.

Brian spoke to Gorrin, "Look, once I've unloaded my shopping, perhaps you could put your new clothes on while I go to the boatyard office and see if that council official is still around."

"Right oh Brian," said Gorrin. "Would you like some lunch?"

Brian turned around to look at Gorrin, "What did you have in mind Gorrin?"

Gorrin replied to this question immediately, "Only some of those delicious sandwiches, that's all. I quite fancy a cheese and tomato, but one not too ripe eh?" He gave Brian a sideways grin as he said this and Brian, grinned back when he realised that Gorrin was thinking about the tomatoes on the bridge.

"That'll be fine Gorrin, I shouldn't be too long in any case, then once we have had our lunch we will be able to get underway and get out on to the Avon." Brian then climbed up the stairway and out on to the deck and Gorrin heard him step out on to the bank.

Gorrin then walked along the deck past the remaining bagged decorative stone, noting as he passed the bags, that about half of the cargo had been removed from the boat, to leave just a few sharp fragments littering the deck. Once back in his cabin, Gorrin opened his carrier bags and took out the various items he had bought in the shop.

He smiled as he held the new purchases up to the light that was filtering though the little round windows in the cabin. Looking at the garments in turn, he chose the maroon shirt and maroon cargo pants, then carefully placed the rest of the unused items into the magic backpack.

The clothes glittered briefly and then disappeared within the bag. Gorrin took off all his old clothes and placed them on to the bed carefully. Quickly he dressed himself in his new clothes and then set about cleaning his old ones.

Opening his green velvet pouch, he took a pinch of the powder and sprinkled it over the clothes singing the cleaning charm song as the fine glittering green faerie dust settled on to the clothing. There was a green sparkling over his clothes for a few seconds and as the light faded, the clean clothes were revealed.

Gorrin folded the clothes and placed them into the backpack and then re-fastened the cover to secure the contents. He returned to the kitchen and began preparing the sandwiches and very soon there were two neat stacks. Then he turned his attention to making a pot of tea.

He picked up his runic staff and pointed it at the gas stove singing the fire charm as he did so. Red light shot out of the end of the staff to strike the gas ring, but nothing happened.

"Rats!" he exclaimed, "Now what's wrong?" Puzzled he looked at the stove and then remembered that he had forgotten to turn the gas on. "Oh you idiot," he scolded himself.

This time he turned the gas on and quickly ignited it with his staff.

Soon the kettle was boiling merrily and its tuneful whistle started, he quickly turned off the gas and made the pot of tea and waited for the return of Brian.

Brian meanwhile had entered the boatyard office and was having an interesting conversation with George the boatyard owner. George was just asking Brian a question.

"Strange thing that was last night with those two thieves. Funny how they were both asleep on the floor, just like a couple of babies, and when we woke them up, they were at a complete loss about how they ended up on the floor in the first place!"

Brian feigned ignorance of these facts as George continued. "And then they both started panicking and saying this place is haunted, what with the books and other things flying about. They both claimed that the place became a real shambles, but by the time we got there, everywhere was spick and span. In fact, I would go as far as to say, it was better than when I left it the evening before."

Brian didn't say anything, but kept on nodding his head in agreement. George continued, "Then, of course, there was that strange thing that happened with the boat slings when it slipped. At least two of my men saw a strange purple light appear in mid-air and it seemed to stop the boat sliding out of the slings and lowered the boat gently to the ground, and then just as suddenly the purple light disappeared."

"Well how very strange!" exclaimed Brian.

"Yes," said George, "I don't suppose you know anything about these things do you?" George implying that he thought Brian did know, but of course Brian wasn't going to admit anything.

At that moment, the door opened and in walked the council official for whom Brian was waiting.

Brian recognised the man immediately as he had a good memory for faces, although his memory for names was less accurate. This newcomer, carrying a leather briefcase, was a small thin-faced man with receding hair and with very pinched facial features. He looked shrew-like and this image was reinforced by the way his small brown eyes darted from one side to the other.

"Well, it's about time you got here," said Brian. "You are from the council, I presume?"

"Yes I am. And you are Mr Brian Yates," replied the official and ignoring the jibe that Brian had made.

"I am," replied Brian, "And I assume that you have my money for the stone I have delivered."

"Of course," said the official, "and in order to complete our business here I need you to sign this paperwork."

"What more paperwork! Huh, you really like to generate lots of paper don't you?" said Brian critically. "It's a wonder that there are any trees left!"

"Really MrYates, sarcasm does not become you. Can you stop criticising our methods and get down to business," replied the council officer.

"Okay, okay keep your hair on," Brian countered.

As he made this comment the thin-faced man stared fixedly at Brian and his eyes narrowed, but he said nothing. Taking out of his briefcase the sheaf of papers, he placed them on to the counter.

"You don't mind if we transact our business here do you," enquired the council official.

"No of course, go ahead," replied George.

Brian picked up the papers and read them carefully before he started to sign them. Although he wasn't happy with the way he had been messed about with his boat cargo, he was not in a position to argue and so didn't say anything. As soon as he had finished signing, the council official presented him with a cheque made out in Brian's name.

Brian thanked him and looked down at the cheque. It was not as much money as he had hoped for, but was still a good profit – so far anyway. He still needed to deliver the other half of the cargo before he could be certain that it was a good return on his labours.

The business concluded, the council officer, said good day and left. Brian watched him as he left with his nose in the air and then turned back to George. "Funny guy that one," he said, "No sense of humour."

And with that Brian said goodbye to George and then left the office and returned to the "Round Tuit" Gorrin was waiting for him with the lunch all ready on the table, together with two mugs of hot sweet tea.

The first thing Brian noticed about Gorrin was that he had changed his clothes for more conventional ones. They really suited him and he told him so. Gorrin was a little embarrassed at this, as he was not used to such praise. Brian then said, "Look Gorrin, they are exactly what you need to wear to blend in. Anyway, I have a couple of presents for you."

Gorrin looked up as Brian said this and replied, "Why Brian, you didn't have to you know."

Brian looked back at Gorrin and said; "Look, you have been a great help and a good companion and friend. If I can help you to fit in to what must be a very different world to the one you left, then that's fine by me."

At this point Brian picked up a carrier bag he had carried back from the shopping trip and presented it to Gorrin.

Inside the bag was a waterproof coat – it was a children's size but fitted Gorrin perfectly as he found out when he tried it on. Looking further into the carrier he pulled out a hard backed book. On its cover was the title 'Journal' and as he opened it inside there was a message, 'To Gorrin, a true and loyal friend, all the very best, Brian.' Clipped to the inside was a writing instrument that Brian had called a biro.

Gorrin looked back up at Brian, and thanked him. He was really quite touched by this act of kindness. Brian said that it was the least he could do. He then sat down and they chatted as they ate the sandwiches.

Brian commented that Gorrin had really got a knack for producing some very satisfying sandwiches. Gorrin replied that he enjoyed cooking and so food preparation was more a labour of love for him, rather than a chore.

It wasn't long before all of the food and tea and been consumed and they sat back to rest for a few moments.

147

Brian said that they had better be getting underway as they still had a fair way to travel before it got dark. Quickly they cleared away and washed up the dirty plates and mugs and went out on deck.

Brian started the engine and a blast of smoke shot out of the exhaust at the side of the boat as it started to run, the vessel throbbing as the diesel engine coughed itself back to life.

Brian cast off the moorings from the bollards and the boat edged away from the bank towards the next lock and the River Avon.

"Just one thing Gorrin," Brian said as they approached the next lock, "please don't use any magic as there will be a lot of people about at the next few locks, and I really don't want anymore attention." As he said this, he thought back to the conversation with George earlier.

"All right Brian," said Gorrin brightly, "if that is what you want."

The sun peeped out from behind a cloud as the boat chugged on towards the next lock with both Brian and Gorrin on deck.

~~~~~~~~~~~~~~~~~~~~~~~

Chapter Eleven
"River Trip"

Their first lock of the day was reached quite quickly and this time, Gorrin climbed up on to the towpath and operated the lock paddles by hand. As he gazed across the lock pound he noticed that a black 53 on a white background indicated the lock number. Gnomes are very strong and their size belies their actual strength.

It was an easy matter for Gorrin to operate the paddle using the windless that Brian had given him. Of course Gorrin would much rather have used his runic staff, but as he has promised Brian to refrain from using magic as much as possible, he had to operate the lock system using brute force.

It wasn't long before they were through the first lock and heading steeply down the lock system and rapidly on to the next one. Finally they were passing under bridge 68 where the canal towpath disappeared completely. This bridge was very low and in preparation Brian had to make sure that there were no pieces of boat equipment standing proud, that might catch on the bridge.

He made a special point to take down the wind generator. Whilst doing this, Gorrin asked why he had a windmill on the boat that didn't appear to be doing anything. Brian explained about electricity and how the wind generator was used to generate top-up power for the battery system. Brian also mentioned the solar panels that he had arranged along the roof of the boat. Gorrin was very interested in how the sunlight could be turned into electricity, although what exactly electricity was, was not clear to him. He made a mental note to enquire about this more deeply later.

They had now reached the point where the canal towpath disappeared completely and as they cleared the bridge, they emerged into a very open part of the canal system. The contrast was astonishing, as one moment they were completely shut away in the canal system and the next moment they were in an un-walled public and very attractive canal basin.

Gorrin looked up to see dozens of tourists looking down at them as their boat hove into view. Many of them held up small boxes to the eyes and they emitted bright flashes of blue white light. For a second Gorrin raised his staff and Brian saw the movement just in time before Gorrin had a chance to start using it.

"Gorrin, its okay, those are cameras they are using, and it's nothing to worry about. All they are doing is taking our picture, just like those in the books." Brian almost shouted this, so nervous was he that his small friend might have done something to attract attention. This was particularly important, as there were so many tourists with camera's and at least one of them would have photographed any public use of the magic staff.

"Well if you are sure," said Gorrin a little uncertainly. Gorrin looked closely at the tourists before he slowly lowered his staff.

"Phew, that was a near one," whispered Brian under his breath.

"Now Gorrin, I think that there is another boat waiting to come up so we will have to wait until they are through the lock before we can enter it," Brian explained to his friend.

Gorrin looked at Brian and then returned his gaze back to the various tourists looking down. "What was that funny name that you used before for these onlookers Brian?" asked Gorrin.

"Oh you mean Gongoozlers Gorrin," replied Brian.

"Yes, that's the word." Gorrin paused then asked: "Why are there so many tourists here at Stratford?"

"Oh that is easy, said Brian, "It's the birthplace of William Shakespeare."

"Oh, well I suppose he was quite famous even in my time Brian. I understand they used to perform some of his plays in a round theatre in London they called The Globe Theatre."

He paused, before continuing: "I never went to the theatre there though. Dirty smelly place London was, with open sewers running along the streets." His mind wandered back in time over the centuries and he remembered that far away time as he said; "I remember last time. I was there walking down one street and someone in a window above shouted, Look out below! And next second an evil smelling liquid descended and covered me from head to foot. I stank for days, before I could get my clothes properly cleaned. At that time I had to be extremely careful that I didn't use magic in very public places, what with all those witch hunts and everything."

"Well yes, I suppose you must have had to be very careful. And you must be careful now, but for different reasons Gorrin," Brian continued; "Now, I think that the lock is now full and those gates are about to open."

Gorrin jumped off on to the side and headed for the lock gates with his windlass. He reached the paddle just as two teenagers reached the paddle system also.

One of the youngsters was a girl and the other her brother.

"Hi" said the girl, "come to give us a hand have you?"

"Yes"-answered Gorrin.

"That's very kind of you, thanks."

"You are welcome," said Gorrin.

As he operated the paddle carefully allowing the water to enter at just the right flow, he turned to speak to the girl, "Where are you headed?"

"Oh, we are on holiday for a week and we are heading for Lapworth and then across to the Grand Union."

"I see," said Gorrin, who of course, didn't, as he was not very familiar with the canal system.

"Where have you come from?" Gorrin asked.

"Oh, Evesham, there's a marina there and that's where we normally moor our boat," replied the girl.

"Well that's a coincidence," said Gorrin, "Because that is where we are headed."

The lock pound was now full and Gorrin and the girl slowly pushed open the lock gate. On the other side, the boy was also opening the lock gate and as both gates opened fully, the canal boat eased its way slowly past to enter the main pound. As soon as the boat was clear, Brian started to move their boat through the gateway into the lock pound, as well. Once the 'Round Tuit' was clear, another boat that was also waiting in the pound followed the 'Round Tuit' into the lock so that they were side by side within the lock itself.

Gorrin had noticed that someone had previously jumped off the boat and was walking around to the lock gate that led on to the river Avon. As soon as the second boat was safely into the lock and secured, both gates were shut and the two paddles lowered.

The girl said that she must go and said goodbye to Gorrin and he in turn wished her a safe and happy voyage. As she headed off along the towpath, Gorrin suddenly thought that he had not even asked the girls name, but then again, she hadn't enquired about his either. "Oh well" he said to himself, "That just the way life goes." And with that he walked over to the other lock gate.

By the time that he had reached the lock gate, the elderly man on the other side was already opening the first paddle. Quickly Gorrin followed suit and soon the water was leaving the lock to enter the Avon very rapidly. As the two levels reached a common point, the pressure on the lock gates eased and Gorrin and the other man were able to open the lock gates.

With the lock gates fully opened, the two now rapidly closed the paddles and waited for the two boats to leave the lock chamber. As soon as they were both clear, the elderly man and Gorrin slowly closed the outer gates until they were firmly shut. That task completed, both Gorrin and the other man headed for the riverbank, against which the two canal boats were now held and roped.

Gorrin climbed on board and then Brian released the mooring rope and the canal boat headed down stream towards its final destination of Evesham Marina.

As they headed downstream, Brian started to whistle and Gorrin joined in once he had memorised the tune that Brian was whistling.

"What's the tune Brian," queried Gorrin.

"Sailing" replied Brian, smiling as he said this.

Gorrin responded with a wry grin and continued whistling.

They cruised along and to their right they passed a very impressive building that was, as Brian informed Gorrin, the Royal Shakespeare Theatre. Onwards they continued and slowly the buildings gave way to some fields with fewer and fewer buildings obvious. Gorrin watched the wildlife as they cruised onwards towards their night mooring at Luddington Lock.

It was not long before they could see the Luddington weir in the distance and as they approached it, Brian made sure that they kept to the right hand side. Eventually they reached the lock pound and Brian manoeuvred the canal boat to the side and proceeded to moor up on the bollards, ready for the night. During the journey, Brian had been listening to the radio and had been studying the clouds and had misgivings about the weather for the following day, but did not say anything to Gorrin.

Meanwhile, Gorrin was an old hand at reading weather signs and had already predicted, at least to himself, that there was likely to be a storm coming soon. He mentioned this to Brian, who though surprised at first, quickly realised that his little friend had many talents besides his magic ones.

Outside the skies continued to fill with cloud and the wind started to rise, while inside the boat kitchen, Brian aided by Gorrin, set about preparing the evening meal. Brian was going to cook a cottage pie and to this he was going to add some vegetables. Gorrin got busy peeling the potatoes, while Brian peeled the onions and cut them up finely. These particular onions were very strong and it wasn't long before Brian had tears streaming down his face, so much so that he could barely see where to cut the onions.

Before he realised it, poor Brian had managed to cut his finger, "Ouch, that hurt," said Brian. Gorrin, of course, came to the rescue with his healing salve that he quickly retrieved from his backpack, just like he had done for the old lady in the department store. The cut was quite bad and the onion juices had managed to get into the cut and were stinging. Brian quickly ran the cut finger under the cold tap to wash away the traces of onions. At this point Gorrin said to Brian; "Come over here Brian, and let me put this special salve on to your cut."

Brian wiped the cut with a piece of clean kitchen roll and applied pressure to stop the bleeding, while Gorrin took a different sheet of kitchen roll and applied some of the salve to the cut. Again the cream seemed to flow around the wound and within seconds the pain was fading fast. A minute or so later and the wound was completely healed. Brian looked carefully at the place where the cut had been and as far as he could see, there was no trace of it.

He looked up at Gorrin and commented, "You know Gorrin, that cream is really very remarkable – I take it that it is magic also."

"Well partly, " said Gorrin, although there are some natural ingredients like honey, beeswax, thyme, woundwort and a few other things, but yes, they only help, the magic unlocks their potential."

"I see," said Brian, "Did you make it yourself then?"

"Yes I did, although about three hundred and fifty years ago though!" Gorrin explained.

"I sort of guessed that you had made it, but I didn't know for sure," Brian continued.

Brian's eyes were still a little sore from the onions, but he made sure that he was more careful this time, when he finished cutting them all up. It wasn't long before they were frying in the pan in a small amount of olive oil. The wonderful aroma of frying onions filled the little cabin and soon Brian was adding the mince and chopped tomatoes. As this was all hissing in the pan, Gorrin walked back over to his backpack and opened it. He called for something that Brian did not quite hear and seconds later a tiny bottle appeared in the pack.

Brian had just added the stock to the pan when Gorrin picked up the small bottle and gave it to Brian. Brian in turn looked at the small bottle critically before saying, "That's very nice Gorrin, but what is it?"

"Why the magic ingredient, Brian," Gorrin replied and he winked as he said this.

Brian looked back at Gorrin, having seen the little wink and wondered whether his little friend actually meant it was magic, or whether it was just a figure of speech and Gorrin was just teasing him.

Brian re-examined the small bottle, inside there appeared to be a liquid but it was completely clear, almost like water, except it behaved more like an oil. Carefully Brian uncorked the small container and peered inside, but he was none the wiser for this. Cautiously he sniffed the contents but it appeared to have no odour. "How strange?" he thought, now what could it be?

He returned his gaze to Gorrin, but all his friend would do was smile in a not quite innocent sort of way. This was frustrating for Brian, but he decided that he would trust his friend, so instead he asked, "Well, how much should I add to the mince then Gorrin?"

"Oh just a couple of drops – no more, otherwise it might spoil the flavour," replied Gorrin.

Brian gingerly deposited two tiny drops into the food and the liquid in the pan immediately seemed to glitter for a spilt second, then the strange effect disappeared. Almost at once, the most incredible aromas started to pour out of the pan. Everything about the food seemed to be somehow exaggerated, but it was difficult to precisely work out what had actually changed.

While the mince continued to cook in the pan, Gorrin finished peeling the potatoes and had started to cut them up into fine pieces ready for boiling. Very soon there was a large pile of pieces of cut potato resting in a dish. "Right," said Brian, "those can go straight into the steamer."

Gorrin looked over to where Brian was pointing and retrieved the electric steamer, placing it on to the work surface adjacent to the cooker. He filled the base of the steamer with water and reassembled it placing the pieces of potato into the top basket and placing the lid on top. Now that the steamer was ready to go, he plugged it into the wall socket and turned the timer round to the fifteen minute mark.

Very soon the steamer was bubbling nicely and the potatoes starting to cook. The meat and tomatoes and seasoning were now ready and so Brian poured them into a large casserole dish. The potatoes were soon cooked and Gorrin removed them from the steamer and passed them to Brian. They were rapidly turned into a fine mash and then placed on top of the, still steaming meat, to form a potato crust. Grated cheese was added to the top, along with a sprinkling of dried herbs and then the whole thing placed under the grill to finish.

They both sat down and continued their conversation while the cottage pie started to brown under the grill. Gorrin began talking about his family to Brian, saying how much he missed them and how he was still wondering what might have become of them in the years when he had slept. A few minutes later, the smell of the cheese just beginning to scorch roused them from their deep conversation and Brian quickly arose to turn off the grill and remove the dish from the cooker.

The food was carefully scooped out of the casserole dish and on to the two plates and as the steam rose into the air, the aromas that they had smelt earlier seemed even more intense. Brian's mouth was watering with anticipation as they both sat down to eat. While the aroma had promised a feast, the actual taste did not disappoint. "That's an incredible flavour Gorrin. In all the years I have been cooking I have never tasted such amazing food." praised Brian.

Gorrin smiled at this then said, "Well Brian, as a sign of my appreciation you can have that bottle, but use it sparingly and not all the time, otherwise you will find it loses some of its potency."

"Are you sure Gorrin?" said Brian.

"Yes, quite sure, in any case I have a few more of those little bottles tucked away in my backpack, so don't worry. It's just my way of saying thank you for all your hospitality."

"Well, Thank you very much Gorrin, but that sounds like you are going to leave. Are you?" Brian queried.

"Soon I will have to, but not until you get to Evesham, then I will have to continue on foot across the countryside," Gorrin explained.

Brian was more than a little sad at this point, as he was going to miss Gorrin. In fact up until Gorrin had arrived, he had not realised that he had become more than a little cut off from other people. While there were many aspects that he liked about his lifestyle, he had begun to realise that he still needed to interact with others, as he was partially gregarious by nature.

Gorrin saw that Brian was a little down at this news, so he decided to give Brian another present. "Brian, there is something else that I can give you, that will help you to get in contact with me, if you need to. Just a moment, I will go and fetch it." Gorrin stood up and walked over to his backpack and opened it. Looking in he called softly for something in a language that Brian did not understand. There was a glow and something appeared in the pack, whereupon when Gorrin withdrew his hand he was holding something.

Brian had been looking at Gorrin and had seen the glow in the pack, but had not actually seen what had materialised. Gorrin walked back to the table and placed a highly polished smoky quartz round stone on to the table. Brian stared at the stone for a few seconds then picked it up and looked at the stones' surface. He could just make out a distorted image of himself staring back at him.

Then Gorrin spoke again, but this time into a similar stone that he was now holding to his face. As Brian continued to look at the stone, the surface appeared to swirl, then clear and suddenly he could see Gorrin's face peering back at him from the stone. He jumped at this and dropped the stone. Immediately, the stone surface went smoky and the image disappeared.

Brian recovered his wits and picked the stone back up and the image of Gorrin reappeared back on the stone surface. As Gorrin spoke, a smaller version seemed to come out of the stone that Brian was now holding. Meanwhile, the stone that Gorrin was holding now had Brian's face staring back at him.

Gorrin explained to Brian how the communicator sun-stones worked. All you had to do was to hold a stone in your hand and call for the name of the person you wanted. If that person had a stone similar to the one you were using, then their stone would vibrate slightly and also glow a yellow colour. As soon as the other person picked up their stone, then each would see the face of the other in their stone. Speech could also be heard, but was a strange tinny version of the original, but was very clear. They were unaffected by distance, but you needed to place them in the sunlight every month or so in order to power them up.

Brian listened to Gorrin fascinated by this until his friend had finished speaking, then he said, "Well, I really don't know what to say, except to thank you for this amazing gift."

"My pleasure," said Gorrin, "Now, I must write up the day's events, a lot has happened today and I have a lot of writing up to do. I think I will start to use that new Journal book you gave me – and I will use that pen that came with it."

Gorrin walked over to the carrier bag where he had left the Journal and picked it up and sat down and began writing. Brian set about clearing up all the dirty crocks and plates, and when Gorrin offered to help, Brian declined saying that he thought that Gorrin should write up his diary. Gorrin queried this, but when it became plain that Brian was adamant on this he sat back down and began writing.

Outside, the wind had begun to blow with ever increasing force and the various birds on the riverbank had all retreated to safer roosts. As the canal boat rocked in the wind, the rain started to fall, splattering across the roof in small speckles at first, then with larger and larger droplets. Soon the rain was hitting the windows making cracking sounds as it hit the glass, then running down in rivulets across the decking.

It was now quite dark outside and the weather was fairly wild outside and it was at this moment that Gorrin decided that he would put on his new waterproof coat and head back to his cabin. As he opened Brian's cabin door, a gust of wind almost pulled it out of his grasp, but fortunately, Gorrin's grip was very strong and he stopped the door from slamming shut.

Gorrin made short work of crossing the deck and entered his cabin. He quickly closed the door and settled down for the night, although since the night was very stormy poor Gorrin did not get very much sleep at all. So he lay awake for the first part of the night listening to the rain hitting the steel roof and feeling the movement of the boat as it moved with the wind. He became vaguely conscious of another movement, but did not understand what this meant until the following day. It was still raining heavily as sleep eventually overtook the very over-tired gnome.

~~~~~~~~~~~~~~~~

Chapter Twelve
"Storm in the Night"

In the early hours of the morning, the strange movement of the canal boat awoke Gorrin, as it rocked back and forth. At first he was not fully aware of what had actually caused him to wake up, until the noise of the heavy rain outside reminded him of where he was. As the memories returned he sat up in bed and listened hard to the rain and the boat creaking, while he tried to determine what it was exactly that had raised him from his dreams.

He looked outside, but the darkness swallowed everything and he could not see much at all, and this was despite his acute vision. He was still troubled and so decided he had better get out of bed and properly investigate. He switched on the bedside light and then quickly pulled on his black boots and his waterproof coat.

167

Resting beside the bedside table was his runic staff. He picked up it up and then tapped it on the deck three times, while he spoke the ancient language of his race. Immediately the runes glowed blue white and then the top of the cane emitted a powerful blue white light that lit up the whole of the cabin – it was far brighter than the feeble fluorescent light from the table lamp.

With the staff firmly held in his hand he opened the door and went outside – and almost immediately the high wind and the driving rain blasted him. The staff, however, blazed its light and the blue-white light penetrated the darkness to reveal the rising water of the river Avon. He looked into the inky blackness with the wind roaring in his ears and checked the boat's position in relation to the bank. It was obvious to Gorrin, that the water level had risen substantially since he had retired to bed and the mooring was a little precarious. The ropes that held the boat were too tight and if they were not let out and the anchor rope was not set properly, then there was a very real risk of the canal boat becoming inundated with water.

Gorrin carefully and briskly walked along the slippery decking to Brian's cabin and rapped smartly on the door, and then promptly opened it. He entered and the blue-white light of his staff lit up the cabin just like a high-powered searchlight. Calling out to Brian, he moved further into the cabin. Gorrin succeeded in waking Brian, although not without some element of grumpiness on Brian's part. One thing Brian did not like was having his sleep disturbed and this was in no small part to the fact that he had managed to consume nearly a bottle of red wine the previous evening.

Brian sat up and rubbed his eyes saying, "What's the matter Gorrin? And does it have to be so bright!"

"It's the boat," Gorrin replied ignoring the comments about the light. "The water level of the river has risen quite a lot, with all of the rain and it's now straining on the mooring ropes. Also, I think the anchor chain has come adrift – or at least it has not been properly set."

At this news Brian's head cleared as the importance of this penetrated his fuzzy thoughts and he got out of bed quickly. Beside the bed were his black Wellingtons and these he pulled on before he stood up. Hanging on a hook on the wall, was a long waterproof coat and this Brian quickly donned and then he picked up his emergency torch. With some semblance of control, he stepped outside and instantly his face was wetted by the cold wind driving the equally persistent rain.

The torch beam was feeble even though it was a halogen bulb, however Gorrin's staff lit up the area just like a carbon arc searchlight, as Gorrin followed his friend out on to the bank.

"Gorrin, I need to release the rope at the stern of the boat, carefully, but before I can do that I need to re-set the anchor chain for safety – after all, we can't have the boat drifting away can we?" Brian shouted, trying to make himself heard over the noise of the rain.

"Right oh," shouted Gorrin back.

Gorrin walked over to where the anchor chain was while Brian grabbed the chain and started hauling it in. He then set the anchor into the bank to prevent the boat from drifting. Rain kept obscuring Brian's vision and he had to keep wiping his eyes to clear them. Gorrin, meanwhile, was holding the staff up high so that it provided as much illumination as it could.

Now that the anchor line was secure, Brian started to untie the stern mooring rope, but unfortunately for Brian, he did not see a root and his foot caught in it so that he lost his balance. Brian hit the ground with a squelch, but his head hit a rock and he was knocked out cold.

Gorrin quickly realised his friend was in trouble and immediately rushed over to see what he could do to help. He looked down at Brian and saw a red stain starting to appear on the side of his head, but as the blood appeared, the raindrops washed it off. Gorrin grabbed Brian under the arms and pulled him away from the edge of the riverbank and then carefully laid him down.

Now Gorrin was in a quandary about what he should do. He had to secure the boat fully but his friend was injured – should he secure the boat first or heal Brian. All the things he needed were aboard the boat, and if the boat was lost, then very probably his friend might be also, as it looked a very serious injury. He came to a decision and it was not one he was comfortable with, but he knew it was one that had to be made under the circumstances.

Gorrin thrust the staff into the ground close to where the mooring rope was tied and then grabbed the mooring rope and untied it giving a little slack to allow for the water to rise. Next, he raced back to the boat and jumped on board, before he headed back to his cabin. In the cabin he opened the backpack and picked up the liniment and the purple velvet pouch, then went outside to where his staff was still standing. Picking the staff out of the ground, he moved over to the prone figure of Brian who was still lying where Gorrin had left him.

Gorrin opened the pouch and dusted himself and Brian with the strangely glittering powder while he sang a little song. There was a 'pop!' and the two figures disappeared from the bank to reappear inside Brian's cabin. Luckily for both of them, they did not materialise inside any walls, decks or other solid objects. They shimmered into view and the blue-white light of the staff immediately lit up the room.

Gorrin put the staff carefully down and picked up Brian and placed him back on to the bed, still in his wet clothes. He examined the bruise now beginning to show as a reddened lump on the side of his head. Gorrin could see the blood was still oozing out but he listened to Brian's breathing – it was slow but regular. "Phew!" said Gorrin. 'At least he doesn't appear to be too badly hurt, but one can never tell with a bang to the head he thought.'

He pulled the jar from his coat pocket, where he had previously placed it and opened it. Taking two fingers he scooped the translucent gel out and applied it to Brian's head wound. It seemed to flow around the site of the bruise and the blood just seemed to disappear, until there was no visible evidence that he had ever injured himself.

As the wound disappeared, Brian gave out a little sigh and visibly relaxed until he was sleeping peacefully. Gorrin removed his wet outer coat and boots, switched off the electric light and then sat in a chair opposite the bed pulling a blanket over him-self to keep warm. Taking the staff again in his hand, he sang a little song in his ancient tongue and the light dimmed until it was almost out – but not quite. He watched Brian for many minutes until he was satisfied that all was as well as could be expected and then closed his eyes as the tiredness overtook him.

Outside the rain and wind continued without even catching its breath and the river continued to rise, although the canal boat was now out of imminent danger. Leaves continued to be blown off the trees and the weather was turning colder. October was just around the corner and Gorrin had a fair way to go until he would reach where he thought his family might be - of course that was pre-supposing that they had not moved in the intervening years.

Morning came slowly as the clouds scudded across the sky and it was a very grey light that filtered through the little round window of the cabin. Brian's consciousness came back slowly as memories of the previous night's events returned to him. Putting his hand up to his forehead, he felt for bruising, but there was none. In fact, as far as he could tell, there was no pain from what had been a nasty impact with a stone, as his head had hit the ground.

He looked across at his little friend who was sleeping peacefully on a chair opposite the bed and he became aware that Gorrin snored – not loudly but enough for him to tell that it was a snore. He sat up in bed, now aware that he wasn't still dressed in his waterproof coat that he had on the previous night, but was nicely tucked up under the duvet.

Getting out of bed he walked over to Gorrin, but as he did this Gorrin came awake almost instantly. The suddenness with which Gorrin awoke surprised Brian and he understood now how lightly the little gnome slept. As an afterthought, it occurred to him that this was why Gorrin had put the sleeping charm on himself in the first place.

Gorrin spoke, "Good morning Brian, I see you have recovered from last night somewhat?"

"Yes, thanks to you I suspect. Although how you managed to get me over to the boat, I suppose you used your magic to do that?" Brian replied.

"I had to Brian," Gorrin apologised, "You are too big for me to lift properly and I certainly couldn't have got you into this cabin without the magic."

"Well I'm glad you did. I suppose you treated me for whatever it was I hit. The last thing I remember is slipping on the grass and seeing the ground coming up to meet me," Brian continued, "Anyway, again I am in your debt. Thank you my old friend."

"Oh, think nothing of it Brian, that's what friends are for." Said Gorrin a little dismissively as he was more than a little embarrassed by all this gratitude.

"Now lets have a look around outside," said Brian.

They went outside and it became obvious that the River Avon was now in flood and travel on the river, at least for today was impossible. It was part of the river code, that when the river was in flood, travel was suspended, until it was safe to do so. The problem was twofold, first there was the problem of the stronger river current itself and secondly, the weirs that were close to the river lock gates were extremely dangerous due to the fast currents. And so here at least for a day, they would have to stay.

They returned to their respective cabins and both got washed and dressed. Soon the breakfast was underway and two hot steaming mugs of sweet tea were sitting on the kitchen table. As they sat down to breakfast, the conversation concentrated on what they were going to do for the rest of the day. Gorrin suggested that Brian rest since although Gorrin had used magic to restore Brian's health, a certain amount of natural rest was still needed. Brian resigned himself to sitting and reading, whilst Gorrin said that he would explore the area a little.

Brian looked hard at Gorrin, as his friend explained what he intended to do and Brian just mentioned that he needed to make sure that he did not use his magic unless it was very important to do so. Gorrin promised that he would only use magic if it was an emergency or only if there was no one watching.

And so it was a little later that Gorrin climbed off the boat and on to the riverbank to explore this interesting new area. The air was very damp and cold and the sky was overcast and grey, but at least it wasn't raining and the wind had died down. The first thing Gorrin decided to have a look at were the two large locks – these were twice as wide as the locks on the South Stratford canal, being able to hold river craft of up to thirteen and a half feet wide. After studying these for a short while he wandered on along the riverbank for a while.

In the distance he could see the village of Welford-on-Avon, but that was too far to walk there in the time that he had this morning, so he decided to study the river for a little while. He noticed that there were parts of it that had not changed much in the centuries since he had last seen the River Avon, but equally, there were other areas that had changed a lot. The rise in the river had caused the river traffic to stop, but as he studied the river, he knew that by tomorrow, they would all be on their journeys again, including the 'Round Tuit'.

He stood for many minutes lost in thought and gazed vacantly at the river, not really seeing it as it was, but rather as it used to be. His mind wandered back in time and he started to think again about his family. He knew that the chances of finding them were probably very slim indeed. The fact that they had not answered his call on the sunstone worried him more than he cared to admit and it was only the busy chain of events that had driven these misgivings from his mind. This time to think was a mixed blessing, but it did give him chance to plan a little more about the journey he was currently undertaking. The biggest worry was that there might be no trace of them at their original location and no hints about where they might have gone. After pondering this for a while he decided that there was no point in trying to *'cross the bridges before he had got to them'* so to speak.

Breaking into his reverie, his thoughts returned to the present and he decided to return to the canal boat as his rumbling stomach reminded him that it was probably lunchtime. It was with mixed thoughts that Gorrin headed back to the 'Round Tuit'.

Gorrin climbed back on board the canal boat and the smell of food cooking wafted up the stairwell from the kitchen galley. This was a most agreeable smell indeed. Brian heard Gorrin climb back onboard and greeted his friend.

"Hi Gorrin, enjoyed your walk?"

"Yes Brian, although it's a bit muddy in places and the river had risen by quite a lot." Gorrin paused before continuing, "I think it has already started to go back down again."

Brian agreed, "Yes I've noticed that the river is already dropping back down, so with a bit of luck we will be able to get underway again tomorrow morning. Now then would you like a cup of tea?"

"Silly question Brian, of course I would love a cup of tea. Now what's that delicious aroma that I can smell?" queried Gorrin.

"Well, that's quite a simple soup I have made from a freeze dried packet, although I have added a couple of extra fresh vegetables," confessed Brian. "I didn't want to go to too much trouble, but then I changed my mind half way through making it."

"Well, I think it will be fine," said Gorrin

Soon they were eating the soup and toast and drinking the tea and since they were both hungry, it wasn't long before they had finished.

"Now what are you going to do this afternoon Gorrin?" asked Brian.

"Well, I thought I would start reading some of those books that we bought the other day, it'll give me chance to catch up on a bit of history." replied Gorrin.

"Good idea Gorrin, it might help to make you a bit better prepared for the world as it is now," said Brian.

So Gorrin and Brian spent the afternoon very sedately, as they both settled down for a quiet read. Every so often, Gorrin would ask Brian a question, prompted by what he had been reading. Sometimes Brian was able to answer and sometimes, he was not, it all depended on the subject.

Outside the weather continued to improve and the wind had almost dropped away completely, while the clouds had thinned and patches of blue sky were making their appearance with increasing frequency. The river, meanwhile, continued to drop back to its normal level for this time of the year.

Evening came and another meal was prepared and eaten and the conversation resumed as Gorrin explained a little more to Brian, about his old life. One thing that became apparent to Brian, during the course of the conversation, was that gnomes were a very secretive people and that they tried their best to keep out of the affairs of humans as much as possible, except for one tantalising fact that Gorrin had briefly mentioned, but had quickly changed the subject when Brian made further enquiries.

It concerned a gnome, who had strayed from the gnome code and had tried to use magic for his own personal reasons. This particular gnome had deliberately meddled with human affairs and Gorrin had given him the distinct impression that this other 'bad gnome' was somehow involved in the spreading of the Bubonic Plague in Oxford, during the English Civil War, sometime during 1642 to 1649.

When Brian had pressed Gorrin for more information, he had only said that they had intervened and prevented any further major incidents ~ except of course during the time just before the Great Fire of London. But as Gorrin was asleep when this happened he could not shed any more light on the matter.

The conversation then moved on to less depressing matters and it was a little later that Gorrin and Brian were sat at the table playing a game of chess. Gorrin had not played for a long time, but this did not seem to matter as he was beating Brian quite comfortably, in spite of the fact that Brian was an ex-county player. Brian was surprised at how good a player Gorrin was, but Gorrin reminded him that he had been playing for many years before he went to sleep.

It was quite late when they finished their fourth game and Brian had managed to win one, but lost three and he had challenged Gorrin to a re-match as soon as there was time. Gorrin agreed to this, but didn't know when this was likely to be.

Gorrin wished Brian a good night and retired to his cabin, but not before he stood looking up at the moon that was now appearing from behind a solitary cloud that had been scudding across the sky. As he looked upwards he noticed a strange bright light in the sky that appeared to be hanging in the heavens and he made a mental note that he must ask Brian about this in the morning. With this last interesting item threading its way through Gorrin's mind, he went to bed.

~~~~~~~~~~~~~~~~~~~~~~

Chapter Thirteen
"Rescue of the Kingfisher"

Next day found the weather had definitely changed for the better, as the morning was clear, with just a few fragments of mist hanging over the river. Gorrin was up early as usual and washed and dressed himself ready for the day. He quickly wrote up the previous day's events in the new journal and then left his cabin and headed for Brian's. As he approached the cabin, he heard the sounds of movement coming from within, so he knocked and entered.

Brian was already making the breakfast, and as Gorrin entered, was just pouring out the hot tea, he looked up at the sound of the door and said; "Morning Gorrin, I thought we should get an early start today, to try to make up for lost time."

"Yes," said Gorrin, "I thought you might want an early start, though I must confess I didn't think that you would be up this early."

"Well, I think we need to get on as the long range weather forecast does not look very good, but there is a break in between the two weather fronts and I intend to take advantage of that. I want to be back on the canals before the next big storm hits," Brian explained.

Breakfast was quickly completed and they cleared away all the dirty dishes in double quick time and then Brian started up the engine. It shuddered back into life and was soon chugging strongly and steadily. Gorrin released the moorings fore and aft and removed the anchor chain and placed all on board, and then jumped back on to the boat. He nearly ended up in the river as his foot slipped and he just managed to grab hold of the railings in time. Brian saw what had happened and quickly held on to Gorrin's arm and hauled him aboard.

"Nearly got a ducking there, eh Gorrin?" said Brian.

"Yes, but thanks to you, I didn't," replied Gorrin.

The river current close to the weir was very strong, as the water was still above normal, although not too high for navigation of the river. Brian had to concentrate on keeping to the right of the weir, until he entered the approach channel for the locks. Soon they were approaching the first big river lock and fortunately for them, there was another narrowboat – the *'Kingfisher'* also waiting to travel downstream. This meant that the heavy task of opening these much larger gates would be shared among the two boat crews.

The lock was quickly passed and they headed on down stream towards the next lock at Welford-on-Avon. Again, Brian had to navigate carefully due to the strong current approaching the weir. The other boat that they were travelling in tandem with was a holiday boat for a family and they were also heading for Evesham Marina. The boat crew consisted of a middle-aged couple, Sam and Barbara with twin daughters Rebecca and Elizabeth, who were aged eighteen. This was likely to be the last family holiday for them as a group, as the twins were off to university in a couple of weeks.

The pairing up of the two vessels was good fortune, as it made the process of getting through the large river locks much easier. During these brief stops, while they waited for the locks to empty and fill, Brian and Gorrin chatted with their new friends. Gorrin and Brian were careful not to mention that Gorrin was a gnome, but they did tell them that this was only a short journey together following the tomato incident.

It wasn't long before they had passed through the Welford lock and were heading on down to the Pilgrim lock. Their day continued, with the water meadows passing to their left and right and their progress along the river was equally swift. All seemed to be going smoothly until they reached the Pilgrim lock. It was at this point that the Kingfisher hit a submerged log causing the shear pin on the propeller to break.

With no power on board to be able to move the boat out of potential danger, the Kingfisher started to drift at a strange angle as it got caught in the strong current that was heading for the weir. The crew could only use the rudder, but this did little to slow the Kingfisher's steady drift towards the weir. In desperation they tried to attract the Round Tuit's crew's attention. Sam wrestled with the boat while Barbara cast the anchor over the side to try to slow the vessels progress towards the weir. Sam hit the boat horn but the sound of the water rushing over the weir made it difficult for Brian to hear the horn.

Gorrin had very sharp hearing and he had been inside the cabin at the time making a cup of tea when he heard the horn. At first he was a little puzzled, as he had not heard many boat horns previously. But, when it was sounded again and again, he realised that it must be something important. As a matter of course, he picked up his backpack and staff and headed up the stair well.

Brian looked down at Gorrin as he appeared in the stairwell and frowned slightly when he saw that Gorrin was holding his runic staff and carrying his backpack.

"Where are you going Gorrin?" enquired Brian.

"I think that the Kingfisher is in trouble – it keeps sounding its horn." explained Gorrin.

Brian quickly turned around to look back at the other boat and after studying the boat for a few seconds he exclaimed: "Oh no Gorrin, something has happened to the boat's power and it is drifting towards the weir. If we don't go and help there could be a nasty accident."

"I don't think we have time to turn this boat around in time before they will be swept on to the weir Brian. I will have to use my magic if we are to stop it." said Gorrin. He opened his backpack and called for the purple velvet pouch.

The inside of the pack sparkled and shimmered and the purple pouch appeared. Quickly, Gorrin withdrew the pouch and dusted himself with a pinch of the strangely glittering powder, singing the special charm in his ancient language. There was an audible 'pop!' and Gorrin disappeared, to reappear a few seconds later on the roof of the Kingfisher.

Meanwhile, on board the stricken canal boat, the two twins had grabbed the life jackets passed two to Barbara and Sam and all were now busily putting them on. The sudden appearance on the roof of the boat startled Sam, as Gorrin just silently shimmered into view and looked straight at Sam.

"How did you?" Sam started to ask, but Gorrin, interrupted him.

"Never mind that now I can discuss it later, but we need to get your boat to safety." Gorrin continued. "Why can't you move the boat out of danger?"

"It's the shear pin on the propeller, we must have hit something in the water and it broke so now the engine runs but the propeller won't go round," explained Sam.

"I see," said Gorrin, "that's easy then," and with that he quickly scrabbled along the roof and hopped down on to the stern deck. Next he opened his backpack and called for the green velvet pouch. Again the inside of the pack glittered and the green velvet pouch appeared, quickly Gorrin removed the pouch and opened it. He took a pinch of the green sparkling powder out.

By now all four of the crew were watching Gorrin intently and their eyes opened wide as they saw the pouch materialise inside the backpack.

"Can you open the engine cover Sam, I need to sprinkle a little of this powder on to it?" requested Gorrin.

"Er. Yes of course, just a minute," said Sam. While he opened the engine cover plate, Elizabeth took the controls.

With a powerful heave, Sam opened the heavy steel cover plate that formed part of the decking. It fell back with a metallic crash on to the deck. Leaning over across the hole in the decking, Gorrin sang the repair charm, while he sprinkled the green glittering powder on to the engine. The engine glittered and sparkled with a green ghostly light and then gleamed brightly as all damage and dirt was removed or repaired.

Vroom! The engine appeared to take on a life of its own, and not a moment too soon. They were now perilously close to the rushing water that was pouring over the weir. Quickly Sam took the rudder and pushed the gearshift forward as far as it would go. The whole vessel shuddered as the power from the engine was transferred into the hull and slowly but surely, the boat pulled away from the weir.

As the boat slowly drew clear from the dangerous maelstrom that preceded the weir, all four turned to look at the small man, who had saved them and their boat from certain disaster.

Sam spoke first: "Gorrin, you have my grateful thanks for saving my family. I will never be able to thank you enough."

Barbara and the twins followed suit with their own thanks, and poor Gorrin who was not used to such praise, went a nice shade of scarlet with the embarrassment.

"Oh, it was nothing, really you know," Gorrin said. "Anyway I must get back to my boat."

"We will take you back Gorrin," said Sam, "In the meantime, please have a cup of tea – or maybe something stronger?"

"Oh no, tea will do fine, sweet and strong please?" Gorrin replied.

Brian had managed to turn the Round Tuit around and was now heading in their direction, but he was too late to assist directly in the rescue, but he had witnessed the green glow of the magic that Gorrin had used to repair the propeller on the Kingfisher. Soon he drew level with the other boat and shouted across to Sam to ask if all was now okay, to which Sam shouted that it was.

A few minutes later when both craft were safely moored at the side close to the lock entrance, Brian was greeted by Sam and invited on board for a cup of tea and biscuits. As he entered the cabin via the stairwell, he looked in and saw Gorrin sitting at a table in what could only be described as canal boat luxury. The inside was fitted with all the latest fittings and furniture. From the side next to the cooker, came the aroma of a stew bubbling in a slow cooker and this inviting aroma filled the air.

Elizabeth and Rebecca were busy questioning his friend as fast as they could get their words out of their mouths and it was Barbara who finally interrupted them saying: "Now, now girls, give Gorrin a chance to speak."

So Gorrin began explaining how he had been asleep and how he had been woken up and how he was looking for his family. The twins saw the look in his twinkling blue eyes as he said this and realised that he was really very sad, but was trying hard not to show it. They both spontaneously gave him a big hug. Gorrin looked up as he saw Brian and smiled and said with a chuckle, "Look at me Brian, two lovely young ladies one on each arm. Not bad for one as old as me, methinks?" They all laughed out loud at this small joke.

It was a little bit of a squeeze for them all to sit around the table, but they managed it. Once they were all comfortable, Barbara invited Brian and Gorrin to come to their boat that evening for an old fashioned stew. Both replied together that they would love to and enquired about the time. Dinner was set for eight o'clock and once they had finished the tea, Gorrin and Brian got up to leave.

Elizabeth who liked to be known as Beth, had been studying the staff that Gorrin had been resting against him. The wood was very dark, almost black and the head was rounded and decorated with strange shapes. Its length was wood that had somehow been braided or twisted on itself and, all in all, it looked more than a simple walking stick.

As Gorrin and Brian got up to go back to their boat she asked Gorrin about it. "Gorrin, those symbols on your staff, they're runes aren't they?"

"You are very observant Beth," said Gorrin. "They are indeed runes, and very old ones at that."

"Is your staff magic as well then Gorrin?" asked Rebecca, whose name was also normally shortened by friends and family to Becky.

"You are quite correct Becky, in fact it is extremely powerful and that also makes it extremely dangerous – at least in the wrong hands," Gorrin added. "Of course, you have to know the appropriate charms to use, otherwise it's just a simple stick. Now I must go as we still have a fair way to go today. We can talk again later if you like."

Rebecca and Elizabeth both almost shouted, "Yes please!"

Now back aboard their canal boat, they continued on through the lock system and on to their next lock at Barton. This lock lay close to the village of Bidford-on-Avon with its rolling hill and meadowland adjacent to the river. Continuing on they reached the next double lock at Marcliff and onward and through the next lock at Harvington Mill. They finally reached their lunchtime destination of George Billington lock at just after two o'clock in the afternoon and after such long haul on the river they were both famished. Brian had prepared the sandwiches, while Gorrin had been steering the boat and so by the time they actually stopped to eat, the food was on the plates.

They both sat munching their sandwiches of cheese and pickle plus ham and tomato and looked out through the window. The sky was no longer quite as clear and sunny as a number of clouds had started to gather, but there was no need to worry just yet, thought Brian.

Gorrin echoed these thoughts out loud and Brian smiled as he said, "You must be a mind reader Gorrin, that's just what I was thinking."

"Well, you know that they say," said Gorrin. "Great minds think alike."

"Or fools seldom differ," replied Brian.

"Mmm, I suppose that to every proverb, there is always it's opposite," responded Gorrin.

Just as they were finishing, the twins from the Kingfisher could be heard coming down the stairwell into the kitchen area.

"You don't mind if we come aboard do you" Rebecca enquired.

"No of course not," said Brian, "I suppose it's not me you have come to speak to, in any case?"

"Rebecca and Elizabeth both looked at each other, "Was it that obvious?" It was Elizabeth's turn to speak now, "We didn't mean to appear rude or pushy?"

"Oh it's quite all right, after all, its not every day, you get to meet a real live gnome, is it Gorrin?"

Gorrin looked across at the two girls and said, "We'll have to talk as we cruise."

They all went back on the deck, but while Brian went to the stern to start up the engine, Gorrin walked forwards to the cargo storage area. There was space to stand now that half of the cargo had been sold and it wouldn't be long before the remaining part of the cargo would leave also. The two girls helped Brian and Gorrin to cast off and then they were able to get underway again.

This was the final stretch before their destination and gave everyone chance to enjoy the river as they chugged along at a steady pace. As they cruised along, the twins quizzed Gorrin about his old life and also about the magic. Gorrin was more than a little careful when it came to talking about the magic and despite the many questions, refused to explain more fully about it. All he did say was of the vaguest of outlines, suffice it to say, that his staff was magic and would perform a number of different tasks, but he firmly declined to demonstrate as he was not one to show off.

Before too long they were approaching Evesham Marina – this was made in record time due to the fast rate of the water flow, since although it was not now in full flood, it was full enough to increase the current. As they swung around in their approach, Brian steered the boat towards a suitable mooring point, to allow for the cargo to be unloaded.

Once securely moored, Brian stepped off the boat and headed for the boatyard office, to arrange for his cargo to be unloaded and also to pick up fuel and pump out the toilet storage system on the boat. Brian arranged this very rapidly and then returned to his boat. It wasn't long before a mobile crane drove to the water edge and the cargo hoisted on to the embankment.

That task complete, Brian moved his boat to another mooring to take on fresh water, pump out the sewage from the holding tanks and fill up with fuel.

As the smell from the pump-out process wafted across the deck, Gorrin's nose wrinkled up and he commented: "Smells just like old London Town did, all those years ago."

The unpleasant smell continued to gather and Elizabeth and Rebecca both decided that they would take their leave and return to the Kingfisher. As they left, they both said: "See you later Gorrin and Brian."

"Well," said Brian, once the two girls had left, "they both seem to have taken a shine to you."

"I had noticed," said Gorrin, "apparently I remind them of their grandfather, who died a couple of years ago."

"I see," said Brian. "They both seemed very interested in your magic staff as well,"

Gorrin, replied, "I think it's the influence of some of your modern films and books,"

They spent the remainder of the afternoon sweeping the decking clear in the cargo hold as quickly as they could, as the nights were beginning to draw in early now, autumn was in full swing. Gorrin looked across to where the setting sun was now only a murky red smudge in the sky and then returned to his cabin to change into a fresh set of clothes.

As usual, before putting the dirty ones away, he used the green faerie dust to clean them, peering into the green velvet bag, his blue eyes twinkled and he smiled at the way the pouch never seemed to empty – but then that was hardly surprising since the pouch was magic also.

Eight o'clock arrived and Brian and Gorrin walked over to where the Kingfisher was moored. Sam greeted them on the stern of the boat. They were ushered inside the boat where they were met by Barbara and the twins.

The table was fully laid for a three-course meal and their hostesses were all dressed in their best canal travelling clothes.

Brian and Gorrin sat where they were directed to sit, with Gorrin flanked by the twins and Brian next to Barbara. Sam sat at the end of the table so that he could, with Elizabeth and Rebecca's help, serve up the starter of prawn cocktail. After this came the beef casserole, with jacket potatoes and finally, the sweet of lemon meringue pie. Red wine was served and Gorrin enjoyed the way the wine complemented the beef casserole.

Conversation surged back and forth throughout the evening and when the conversation finally came to an end, Gorrin said how he had enjoyed being asked out to dinner and thanked them all. Brian, of course reinforced this, with his thanks and it was well past midnight by the time they returned to the 'Round Tuit'.

Back on board and finally in his cabin, Gorrin decided to write up the day's events before retiring to bed. During the course of the evening's conversation he had indicated that tomorrow he would have to say goodbye to Brian and continue his journey alone. Of course Brian was aware that this was to happen, but he had got used to having his little friend as a travelling companion. Sad as he was to see him go, he knew it was inevitable.

Gorrin replayed the events of the day in his mind and he quickly scribbled down the details in his journal until he had finished. As soon as he had finished he went out on deck once more to look up at the strange bright light in the sky that seemed to be following the moon.

A short while later he slipped under the bed covers. His last waking thoughts were that he really must ask Brian what the strange bright white light was in the sky.

~~~~~~~~~~~~~~~~~~~~~~~

Chapter Fourteen
"Back On the Road Again"

The morning mist hung heavily over the river as the first rays of light crept across the land, penetrating the gloom slowly but surely. Gorrin awoke as this almost ghostly light filtered through the curtains in his cabin. Gorrin's consciousness returned and his thoughts turned to the fact that today was when he must continue on his journey alone and leave his friend Brian behind. While this saddened him, since he had a lot to thank his friend, for Gorrin realised that this was inevitable, if he was to continue his search for his family.

Outside, he could hear the water lapping against the hull of the boat and the occasional quack of a passing duck. He quickly got out of bed and washed and dressed himself before leaving his cabin. He had packed his things into his backpack the previous evening and so he picked up his backpack and runic staff and headed for Brian's cabin.

He noticed the heavy dew that glistened on the metal surfaces of the boat, as the sun's rays continued to light up the scene. He fixed these images into his mind and continued along the deck until he reached Brian's cabin and politely knocked. There was no answer, so he knocked again, but still silence greeted him – well almost, because as he listened, he could plainly hear the steady snoring of his friend.

Quietly he opened the cabin door and stepped inside and looked across at Brian who was still sound asleep. He put down his backpack and using his staff ignited the gas burner and started making the tea and preparing the breakfast. This morning, he was going to have porridge made with milk and a small amount of honey to sweeten it. It wasn't long before the tea was poured and the porridge was sitting in two bowls, with the steam gently rising into the cool air in the cabin.

He gently woke Brian from his slumbers but this was not an easy thing to do as his friend had slept very deeply. The previous day's events, as well as the altercation with the injury had taken their toll. Brian's eyes flickered open and they slowly focused on the small figure that stood beside him. He noticed that Gorrin was holding a mug of hot tea and a biscuit.

Brian's awareness sharpened and he sat up in bed and took the offered cup and biscuit and mumbled his thanks. Sipping the hot tea helped to bring his thoughts into clearer focus and the realisation that this was the day that Gorrin was to move on to continue his quest to find his family.

"Well Gorrin, are you ready to continue on your journey to find your family?" queried Brian.

"Yes, Brian" replied Gorrin. "Anyway, unless you have forgotten, you can always see and speak to me using the sunstones."

"Oh yes, I had forgotten," confessed Brian.

Gorrin continued when his friend went silent, " Now, come and eat your breakfast, it'll get cold if you leave it too long."

Brian climbed out of bed and sat down at the small kitchen table and started to eat the porridge. "Mm this tastes absolutely delicious Gorrin," said Brian then he looked directly at Gorrin, It doesn't have an added magic ingredient does it?" enquired Brian pointedly. "How did you guess?" replied Gorrin and he smiled a sideways smile, "Anyway it's not quite the same as the one I have given you, but very similar."

Gorrin then joined Brian in eating his breakfast and it wasn't long before they had both finished.

"Brian, there's something I've been meaning to ask you" said Gorrin. "What's that very bright light in the night sky, it's smaller than the moon but very bright and it moves quite fast across the sky. It's not a star so what is it?"

"Oh, you must mean the International Space Station," explained Brian.

"What's that?" asked Gorrin. So Brian spent the next ten minutes trying to explain what it was.

Gorrin accepted it, but was more than a little puzzled as to why people should want to go up into space in the first place. Brian then explained about how they were just explorers and that a lot of inventions had been produced as a result of the research. Gorrin was fascinated by this and kept on asking Brian many questions.

Finally, Gorrin decided that he should probably stop asking so many questions and let Brian get dressed in peace. He stood up and indicated to Brian that he was going out on deck to have a look around while Brian got washed and dressed.

Outside the day was cool and cloudy and the mist was still hanging over the river and Gorrin spotted a couple of swans gracefully swimming past. The two swans looked across at the little figure who was quietly observing them. They paused briefly as if to say good morning and Gorrin nodded back and wished them both a good morning, after which the two continued on along the river.

He now looked across at the 'Kingfisher' and could just see the first signs of movement as Sam appeared on deck. Sam caught sight of Gorrin and waved at him and Gorrin climbed off the boat and walked along the riverbank towards the other boat.

"Good morning Sam," greeted Gorrin.

"Morning to you too Gorrin," replied Sam. "Are you ready to leave then?"

"I am, but I was waiting for Brian to get dressed before I left – he's still a bit tired from the other day but he's on the mend I think. I will tell him to rest for a day or so before he heads back, although I know he wants to be back on the canals before the next big storm comes."

Sam nodded and said, " We are not leaving straight away as we have to unload quite a lot of things into our car – we over-winter our boat here and I have various things I must do before we leave. This year the boats got to be lifted out to check the anodes and the hull. So we can keep an eye on him for a day or so"

"Thanks for that Sam; at least he won't think you are trying to be a mother hen too much. He has been saying since he had his little bump that I have been fussing too much, but I suppose that it's a sign that he is fine now."

Below the deck there was a sound of more movement and two heads appeared in the stairwell. Gorrin recognised them immediately as Rebecca and Elizabeth. "Hello Girls" greeted Gorrin, "Bit early for you to be up and about isn't it?" remarked Gorrin, with a smile on his face. They both indignantly objected, until they saw the grin and realised that the gnome was teasing. They both continued in mock indignation, but they were only play-acting and very soon were laughing.

Barbara now joined them on deck and greeted Gorrin with a hot steaming mug of tea and Gorrin thanked her and took the offered mug and sipped it. They discussed a little more of Gorrin's journey plans and Barbara asked Gorrin to excuse her for a minute while she went to fetch something.

She was soon back holding some sandwiches that she had made and a whole armful of other food items for his journey. He took his leather backpack off and opened it and placed all of the items into the pack. The items sparkled and shimmered and then disappeared until all you could see was an apparently empty pack. The twins and Barbara and Sam saw this and all were surprised at the way there was nothing left in the pack.

Elizabeth asked, "Gorrin, where do all of the things go to?"

"Well," said Gorrin, "they haven't really disappeared; they are all there, just not at the same time." explained Gorrin.

Elizabeth was intrigued with this, "Do you mean they are out of phase with each other?"

"I don't know that word," said Gorrin, "But they all occupy the same space but in different planes of existence."

"That's amazing!" said Elizabeth and Rebecca together.

"Well I think so," said Gorrin, "Anyway, that's enough of that now, I must get back to the Round Tuit as I see that Brian is now dressed."

Gorrin had noticed that Brian was now on deck and looking for him. He wished them all a goodbye and thanked them for their kind gifts and the twins and Barbara gave him a big hug and kissed him. Gorrin, of course, went a lovely shade of scarlet at this but his blue eyes twinkled. Sam came over and they shook hands and Gorrin turned back to his pack that was still sitting on the deck.

He quickly shouldered his pack and walked back over to Brian's boat where his friend was waiting for him.

"Now Gorrin, I have got you something for your journey, which I hope you will find very useful." Brian now picked up a cylindrical parcel and stitched on to the side was a label. The label gave a clue to the contents as it said *'Two Person Tent – Rapid Assembly'*.

Gorrin was speechless for a few seconds and then said, "Brian, that's a very kind thought and I will find that very useful in the coming week, of that I have no doubt."

"My pleasure, anyway it's not very new, I bought it last year, but its never been used and I think that you are much more likely to use it than me, don't you think?" explained Brian.

"How do you assemble it Brian?" asked Gorrin.

"Oh it's very easy," said Brian, "look I'll show you."

Brian quickly unpacked the tent and within a couple of minutes a small dome tent was soon built. Almost as quickly Brian disassembled it and packed it away. Now it was Gorrin's turn, and at first he managed to nearly poke himself and Brian in the eye more than once with the plastic poles.

Gorrin continued the assembly and disassembly until eventually he had mastered the process. Happy with his efforts, Gorrin re-opened his backpack and placed the tent inside, which glittered briefly, and the tent shimmered then disappeared. Brian had gone back inside the boat and returned with a plastic bag full of provisions for Gorrin's journey, which he handed to Gorrin.

"For your journey – just a few things I've put together," explained Brian. He removed a map and compass from the carrier bag and handed them both to Gorrin. "I picked those up in Stratford, as I thought you might find them useful."

Gorrin tucked the map and compass into his jacket pocket.

"Thank you Brian," replied Gorrin, and he placed the carrier into his backpack and then closed the pack and hefted it on to his back.

"I take it you know all about how to use a compass and read a map Gorrin?" queried Brian.

"Yes, of course," said Gorrin, "We gnomes have been using a compass and maps for years, long before you humans 'discovered them. Who do you thing gave you the idea in the first place?"

Brian's eyebrows went up at this and he said: "Are you serious Gorrin?"

"Oh yes perfectly," replied the gnome.

Gorrin was dressed in his waterpoof jacket and cargo pants and woollen hat and said, "Many thanks for your hospitality and your friendship." He shook Brian's hand warmly as he said this, his blue eyes twinkling and a look of sadness playing at the edges of his eyes.

"It's been a real pleasure. After all, who can say that they have met a real live gnome - and anyway, I don't suppose anyone would believe me anyway." Brian chuckled as he said this and continued: "Seriously though, please stay in touch Gorrin, I will give you a call with the sunstones and you can let me know how you are getting on and what adventures you have had."

Then as an afterthought, he added a warning to his gnome friend. "Just remember though, people won't have seen real magic before and you don't want to attract unwanted attention by using it in a public place where lots of people can see it."

"All right Brian, I'll remember," replied Gorrin.

With that, Gorrin turned and with his runic staff in one hand and his backpack securely in place, he began to walk away from the marina and headed off across the fields.

In the distance across the fields he could hear the sound of a trains clattering along the railway line on its way south. Gorrin thought to himself, "That's the direction I have to go." And he continued on his journey across the damp wet fields until he came to a large road along which cars were speeding towards the Cotswolds. He decided that it looked much too dangerous to walk along the road, so he decided that he would follow the road but from the safety of the fields.

The branches of the hedgerows that bordered the road were dripping with the early morning dew still and the overcast grey day was only gradually clearing. Several hours had passed before the weather appeared to improve and the sun started to break through and burn off the damp mist that still clung to low lying areas.

Mid morning came and Gorrin decided to have a break so he sat down on a nearby log and opened his backpack and sang for the item he wanted. A sparkle appeared inside the pack and the carrier bag Brian had given him appeared. He reached inside and pulled out a couple of small plastic drinks bottles and a chocolate caramel bar. Closing the backpack caused the carrier bag to disappear again. He sat munching on the chocolate bar and drinking the apple juice. The other bottle he tucked into his jacket pocket.

As he sat on the log, he cocked his head to one side and listened to the sound of the cars speeding past. He pursed his lips and said out loud, "Such a hurry people are in, how the world has changed." He finished his drink and put the empty bottle into one of his other pockets. Getting up off the log he set off again towards his next destination of Moreton-in-Marsh.

~~~~~~~~~~~~~~~~~

Chapter Fifteen
"The Lost Dog"

Gorrin continued walking along the side of the hedgerow that lay beside the main road noting the scenery around him as he walked along. The most obvious change to him that seemed to have occurred was the size of the fields, whether they were just pasture or planted with crops. They were many times larger than when he had been last in the country and the hedgerows had a wider range of trees within them. The other point was that there seemed to be less insect life – although at this time of year that was difficult to gauge as it was now well and truly autumn and heading rapidly towards winter.

He was well into the Vale of Evesham and various winter crops had been planted, such as winter kale and potatoes, but most of the fields had just been ploughed under to allow the cold weather to break down the soil, ready for spring plantings.

After he had been travelling for a couple of hours, he decided to check the map and use the compass to get his bearings. He found three landmarks on the map and took compass bearings of them. By back tracking along the line he was able to triangulate his position and so pinpoint his actual position on the map. He was quite impressed with the compass as it was lightweight and had a magnifying lens built into it. Brian had explained that it was what they called an *'Engineer's Compass'* and that it was military in origin. Despite this, however, he did mentally congratulate the human who had designed it - as it was quite ingenious.

Now that he knew exactly where he was he decided that it was probably time for lunch ~ this he reasoned was due in no small part to the feel and sound of his stomach that was now rumbling quite loudly. He took off his backpack and opened it and called for a water bottle and the packets of soup. As these items glittered and appeared within the pack, he realised that he needed a pan to heat the water in. He paused for a few seconds then he remembered that he had packed a number of these when he had left his home in the woods.

He called for a saucepan, and as before, the pan appeared in the pack. He removed this and set about putting water in the pan ready for the fire. Brian had packed some matches that he described as waterproof, but Gorrin decided that he would use magic, as it was easier. Before he could do this, however, he needed to gather together some kindling and larger pieces of wood for the fire.

Soon he had gathered a nice small wigwam of wood with two large branches either side of it. He pointed his walking staff at the fire, and was about to sing the fire charm when he remembered his promise to Brian. He looked around to check for anyone watching and as soon as he was sure that no one was about, he sang the fire charm. The runes around the top of the cane glowed red and a red beam of light sprang from the end of the cane towards the wood. Despite being damp, it burst into flame and started crackling and spitting sparks.

Quickly he placed the saucepan of water across the two logs and settled down to watch the pan boil, for there was little else to do, or so he thought. But, as he gazed into the flames, he remembered that he had forgotten that he had plenty to read. He retrieved the book on the 'History of Costume' and started to read. He became so engrossed in the book that he forgot his hunger – that was, until his stomach rumbled so loudly he thought it might bring someone to investigate the noise.

It was the sound of water boiling over into the fire and hissing into steam that roused him from his book and he placed the book down and set about pouring the water into a tin mug to mix with the dried mushroom soup. Stirring the soup and hot water mixture with a spirtle that was normally used to stir porridge, he was interested to see how quickly the mixture thickened and turned into a nice thick soup.

The steam from the hot soup rose into the air and hung about before thinning and disappearing. Gorrin slowly sipped the soup, but managed to burn the roof of his mouth, as the soup was still very hot. Indeed it was really too hot to drink. "Ouch, Rats! That's hot," exclaimed Gorrin to no one in particular.

He found the cup of hot soup very filling and tasty, indeed he recognised the fungi in the soup as being what used to be known as a *'Penny Bun'* with a most delectable flavour. The soup eventually cooled sufficiently for him to sip it without burning his mouth and he decided to continue reading his book, whilst he sipped his soup.

He did not notice that overhead a few heavier clouds had gathered and very soon the first large raindrops started to fall. Splat! one landed right in the middle of the page he was reading and this caused him to look up. 'Splat', another landed this time right in his eye, which he promptly screwed-up as the rain was icy cold.

Gorrin quickly studied the sky and decided that it was an ordinary storm and not a thunderstorm and so he thought that there was likely to be no problem with using any trees as cover, until the rain had blown over.

Picking up his backpack and putting it on his shoulder, he retrieved his runic staff and tucked it into his belt, and with his mug of soup headed for the nearest tree – it was a holly bush and while providing good cover from the rain, it was very prickly and he suddenly wished that it was a different tree as he was getting quite scratched.

The rain came down stronger and he huddled under the tree still sipping his now rapidly cooling mug of soup. Gorrin now had a choice; he could either remain where he was sitting and get scratched, or he could move from under the tree and get wet. He decided to remain where he was sitting, but started to regret this decision as he felt a number of prickly holly leaves sticking into his rear end.

The rain was now running in small rivulets across the broken soil and around the remaining clumps of grass. Since his soup mug was now empty, he decided to use the rain running off the holly leaves to rinse out his cup.

He sat cross-legged on the floor for about half an hour, then the rain finally eased until there were only a few raindrops falling. Finally, it stopped raining and the sun began to break through the clouds. His breath was now steaming in the air as the rain had caused the temperature to drop several degrees. He got to his feet and struggled out from underneath the holly tree. Once out in the open he removed several dried holly leaves that had been sticking into his rear end and pulled a face as they came out, "Ouch, that hurt" Gorrin said out loud.

He walked over to the fire that was now extinguished by all the rain and sprinkled some of the repair powder over the ashes and sang the charm. The green sparkling powder shimmered over the ashes and within seconds grass had sprouted. Soon there was no evidence that there had ever been a fire there.

Gorrin studied the scene for a few seconds, and satisfied with what he could see, turned and walked away. He stopped in his tracks when he realised that he was still holding his soup mug. He placed the mug into the backpack, pulled the staff from his belt and set off once again parallel to the trees and the road.

Meanwhile, Richard, Michael and Stephen were all busy looking for their dog who had successfully given them the slip and headed off chasing pheasants across the fields when they had been climbing trees and walking along one of the many paths that criss-crossed the landscape.

Stephen, the eldest at 14 years, was very tall for his age and was frequently mistaken for being much older. He was now busily accusing Michael, his younger brother of being careless with the dog lead. "Look, if you had done what I told you, none of this would have happened."

"But I did tie it properly to the tree when we went climbing up that big old oak," defended Michael. He was the middle of the three brothers and was also quite tall for a twelve year old and wasn't afraid to stand up to his elder brother.

The youngest of the three was Richard and all that he could keep on saying was, "We have lost our Lucky!" Richard loved animals and it was his great fondness for the family dog that made him very upset that his favourite animal had managed to run off across the fields.

Stephen was now trying the old tactic of trying to make Michael feel guilty by saying: "If we don't find him soon, one of the farmers might shoot him as a stray – don't forget that there are flocks of sheep about and they don't like lone dogs roaming around."

This had the desired effect on Michael, as a look of extreme panic now crossed his face and he exclaimed, "Oh no, I had forgotten about that! We really must find him quickly."

Stephen had seen the look on Michael's face and thought that his comments had achieved the desired effect, so he continued; "It might be worse, Lucky might have fallen down an old well."

This new thought panicked Michael still further and he was about to voice his worry when Richard started calling "Luck…y, Luck..y" as loud as he could. Michael joined in and soon so did Stephen. They continued calling and walking until they spotted a lone figure coming towards them. The figure was a child wearing green clothing and was moving in their direction at a fairly brisk pace. Michael then said, "Maybe that kid has seen Lucky. I think we should ask him."

"Yea okay," said Stephen, "That's probably a good idea." And so the three continued shouting their dog's name and walking towards the distant figure.

Meanwhile, Gorrin had been travelling for a couple more hours when he heard the sounds of three people calling out in the distance. His ears pricked up at this as he strained to hear what was being shouted. The sound was at least half a mile away so whoever was calling must have been shouting as hard as they could.

Gorrin could just make out the word and it sounded like *Lucky*, but the wind kept whipping the word away. As he drew nearer he became certain that they were definitely calling out the name 'Lucky'.

His sharp blue eyes caught sight of the three figures that were all calling out the name he had heard. The three figures were children, but two of them were very tall, in fact two of them were a lot taller than Gorrin and the third was about Gorrin's height and they were walking directly towards the gnome.

As the three boys drew nearer to the small child they had been watching walk towards them, they noticed that it wasn't a small child at all, but a rather short old looking man with a silvery grey, short, pointed beard and silver grey hair peeping out from a woollen hat. But the most noticeable thing about him were the very bright blue eyes that appeared to twinkle. The little man was holding a rambling stick and as they got closer they saw that the stick was very ornate.

Stephen spoke first as he was the eldest. "You haven't seen a black and white dog have you, only we've lost ours."

Gorrin paused for a few seconds and then responded with a greeting. "Good afternoon." Then he looked pointedly back at the three and didn't say anything else.

Finally Richard said; "Good afternoon mister. We've lost our dog and I am scared that he may be hurt or trapped or lost or…" Richard continued rambling on, as he was quite distressed.

Stephen then said, "Yea, afternoon. Look mate, you haven't seen a small black and white dog, only my brother here managed to lose it." As he said this, he looked directly at Michael.

Gorrin listened to their tale and then said, "No I haven't seen a dog of any kind, but that doesn't mean to say he is not around somewhere. I might be able to help, but first I think we should introduce ourselves, "he paused slightly and added, "as it's the polite thing to do, isn't it?" He then looked pointedly at Stephen, who promptly blushed slightly.

Stephen was not one to be embarrassed normally, but this strange little man who seemed to radiate a sort of no nonsense authority and this was at complete odds to the small man's outward appearance.

Stephen then collected his thoughts together and said, "Er sorry. I didn't mean to be rude, only my dad will hold me responsible if we lose Lucky, as I am the eldest. Good afternoon, my name is Stephen and this is Michael and he's Richard." He pointed at his two younger brothers as he said this.

The gnome replied, "Well, good afternoon to you boys, my name is Gorrin and I am travelling south looking for my family."

Stephen looked at Michael and he returned the look as Gorrin said this and Michael then said, "You walking then?" Of course, this was pretty obvious that Gorrin was walking, but the way he had said it implied that he had been travelling some distance. And from his clothing, which although it was a bit mud spattered, the small man didn't look like the typical tramp.

Richard, the youngest had no problem with asking: "Are you a tramp mister?"

Gorrin was a little taken aback at this directness, but he quickly recovered and answered, "No Richard, I am not a tramp, I just travel on foot as I don't have any other transport. " He paused and then went on, "Now, tell me more about your lost dog?"

Stephen then went on to explain how they had taken their dog for a walk and had been exploring a copse when they had found a large oak tree that looked inviting from a climbing point of view. They had then tied up Lucky at the base of the tree, while they had started to climb as high as they could, as it was very tall and quite easy to climb. They had been almost at the top of the tree, when a pheasant had wandered past and Lucky had given chase pulling the lead with him.

Since Michael had not tied the knot to a secure branch, the rotten branch to which it had been tied had snapped and off into the distance Lucky had bolted. The pheasant meanwhile, had, of course, scampered across the ground before taking to the air and flying away at low level. This had just teased their dog and he had given chase into the distance. Now they did not have a clue as to his actual whereabouts and so were searching for him.

As Gorrin listened intently, he nodded as the story was related, until Stephen had finished, at which point he said; "Well boys, I think I may be able to help, but first I need something that belongs to Lucky."

"What do you need something of Lucky's for?" asked Michael.

"Well, it's a little bit of what you might call magic." replied Gorrin.

"Oh yes, pull the other one," countered Stephen, who was plainly sceptical about the use of magic.

"Look, Stephen, you have everything to gain and nothing to lose, as it's obvious you still have no dog?" Gorrin explained.

"I have a small rubber squeaky bone that is Lucky's favourite toy," replied Michael. He thrust his hand into a coat pocket and pulled out a rather battered rubber bone that was well bitten and gave it to Gorrin.

"Thank-you," said Gorrin. Then he pulled out of his inside coat pocket the map he had been using and opened a small pocket in the top of his coat and pulled out a small crystal attached to a silver chain.

Stephen asked; "Well, what are you going to do then?"

"Patience and a little quiet please," admonished Gorrin. "I need to concentrate."

Gorrin then spread the map out on the ground and held the crystal and chain by his right hand, while holding the rubber bone in his left hand. He relaxed his mind and started to think only of the dog.

The crystal on the chain started to move - only slightly as first, but then it started to rotate in a clockwise direction. The rotation continued and Gorrin moved the crystal across the map until the circles got tighter and the motion increased until its pointed end stopped over a strange marking on the map.

The three boys had been watching this with great interest, although for Stephen, it was more scepticism than interest. Richard asked a question, "What that called Gorrin?"

"Oh, it's nothing special, some call it dowsing others call it scrying, it just depends on who is telling the story," explained Gorrin to the three boys.

Gorrin carefully examined the map at the point where the crystal had come to rest. Then he said, "That's where lucky is, and if I am not mistaken there is a house there."

Stephen and Michael peered over to where Gorrin was pointing on the map and they both said together, "There's no house there, only a few piles of bricks."

"Well that's where we should start to look," replied Gorrin.

"Are you sure?" questioned Stephen, "That wasn't the direction that Lucky ran off to."

"Quite sure," asserted Gorrin.

"Okay," said Stephen, who was still very sceptical about this strange procedure that Gorrin had just carried out.

And so they headed towards the place on the map that Gorrin had pointed to. It was about half a mile across the fields to the ruins of the old house. There was little of the building remaining and what was visible was largely overgrown by ivy grass and brambles. The three boys started to call out for their dog. At first when they listened, only silence reached their ears. They continued to call, and Michael and Stephen looked at Gorrin who was now listening intently.

"Please stop shouting," said Gorrin, "I need to listen for your dog."

They all went silent and listened, Gorrin suddenly exclaimed, "I can hear him whining and he is quite close to where we are at the moment."

They all listened again, but only Gorrin could hear the plaintive noise that Lucky was now making. The poor dog had been scrambling over the ruins and, in trying to catch the pheasant, had run over a section of ground that had collapsed down into the old cellar of the ruins. The rubble had then closed over the entrance and trapped the dog below the ground in a very small pocket.

Lucky had been whining and feeling very sorry for himself, when he had heard the cries of his owners. He had then redoubled his efforts to attract their attention. Fortunately for Lucky his cries had been heard by the sensitive hearing of the little gnome.

Gorrin listened carefully for where Lucky's cries were coming from. At first he was not sure, then as Lucky gave another loud whine, he managed to pinpoint where he believed the dog to be trapped. Gorrin carefully walked over, picking his way carefully through the loose rubble and walked over to a hole in the ground that was partially covered by undergrowth. He was very careful not to dislodge anything else, but Stephen was not so cautious and he blundered across towards the hole. In his haste, he stumbled across some loose rubble.

It happened in a flash, one second he was standing there and the next moment, he had stumbled forward and he disappeared, the ground appearing to open up like a monster's open mouth. He disappeared down the dark hole in the ground, giving a brief and startled cry. With a look of horror frozen on their faces, the two remaining brothers and Gorrin saw him vanish as if the very ground had swallowed Stephen up and a deep silence descended on the scene.

~~~~~~~~~~~~~~~~~~~

Chapter Sixteen
"Rescued From the Cellar"

As the silence descended over the scene, a fine dust rose as if to mark the spot from where Stephen had disappeared. The silence was broken by Michael's extreme agitation at the sudden disappearance of Stephen, "Gorrin, whatever shall we do?"

Gorrin answered quickly; "Stop exactly where you are, and don't take any further steps, we don't want anyone else to vanish, do we?"

The two remaining brothers nodded and a look of consternation crossed their faces as they looked around at the ground, suspiciously, waiting for the ground to swallow them up also.

A few seconds passed and these seemed to hang in the air for a long time before it became clear that no further movement was happening with the ground. Gorrin then spoke again, "Now boys, both of you, carefully try to retrace your exact steps away from the hole, but do it slowly and very carefully."

Michael and Richard gingerly retraced their footsteps as closely and carefully as they could, until they were several metres from the place where Stephen had disappeared. Gorrin, meanwhile had been carefully listening for any tell-tale sounds that Stephen had survived the collapse of the ground, but the heavy breathing of the two boys close by was making this particular task very difficult.

Gorrin spoke to the two saying: "Now then lads, don't worry, I need you to move away a little further so that I can listen for Stephen – and Lucky of course."

The two boys looked at each other then back at Gorrin and finally the place where Stephen had disappeared.

After staring for a few seconds they both solemnly nodded and they moved further away. Now that they were further away from the area, Gorrin could now listen for the sound of Stephen and Lucky. Straining his hearing he could just make out the steady, but faint breathing of Stephen and this was mixed with the much faster panting of Lucky.

He looked back at Richard and Michael and with relief showing on his face said: "Boys, I can hear both your brother and the dog breathing quite steadily. That's good news at least. Now we have just got to get them out."

"How are we going to do that?" exclaimed Michael.

"Why magic of course!" replied Gorrin, with a glint in his blue eyes.

Gorrin pointed his staff at the rubble where Stephen had been moments before he disappeared down into the ground and began to softly sing a very ancient song. The runes on the staff began to glow purple, only faintly at first, then brighter and brighter, until they were blazing a very deep amethyst purple.

From the end of the staff came a beam of purple light and this Gorrin waved over the rubble and then focused it on to a patch of grass well clear of where the boys were standing. The two boys meanwhile stood transfixed by the sight of this amazing light show and their jaws dropped in surprise as the first of the bricks and rubble rose into the air and headed for the point where the beam of purple light was focused. At first, only a few small pieces of rubble moved, but more and more started to rise into the air until larger and larger pieces of brickwork and soil were rising and rapidly moving through the air to land on the ground ten metres from where they had started.

Gorrin continued to sing concentrating all his thoughts on the process of excavating a large hole around where

Stephen and Lucky lay trapped. Richard and Michael could not believe what they were seeing and yet, in a way, the sight of this strange little man wielding this magic seemed completely in character with what they had witnessed so far. Both wondered where Gorrin had come from – it seemed the stuff of fairy tales and yet here, right before their eyes, magic was indeed being used.

It was not long before a sizable hole had opened up in the ground and Gorrin could see the figure of Stephen lying in what appeared to be an old brick built cellar. Stephen was obviously unconscious and partially covered with soil and pieces of brickwork. Lucky on the other hand, was glad to be free of the brick prison and struggled up the sides of the hole and headed straight for Richard and Michael.

Both the boys were overjoyed to see their dog, but this joy was tempered by the fact that they could not see Stephen from where they were standing. Both boys started to move forward towards the hole, but Gorrin quickly waved them back, shaking his head and frowning, as he continued his soft singing.

Both boys froze again as they understood what Gorrin meant and they carefully retreated back. Richard then started to pat and generally fuss their dog, while Michael made secure the dog lead. He was not about to risk losing the dog a second time in one day.

Gorrin now stopped singing and the staff promptly stopped projecting the purple light. He pointed the staff at Stephen and started to sing again, only this time the song was a slightly different version of what he had just been singing. Gorrin then pointed the staff at a place close to where the two boys were now standing and this scared the two boys at first, until they realised what Gorrin was actually doing.

Gently rising out of the cellar Stephen floated upwards and then towards where the runic staff was now focused. The two boys both beamed with relief as they saw their brother floating out of the hole and across towards where they were standing. As Stephen floated along, it became obvious that one of his legs was twisted at a strange angle.

Gently, Gorrin lowered the still unconscious figure of Stephen to the ground and ceased his singing. The purple light winked out and the runes on the staff ceased to glow. Gorrin then carefully walked over to the three boys, picking his way through the debris on the grass until he reached where Stephen was lying. He bent down and listened to Stephen's shallow breathing and then studied the leg that was obviously broken.

Stephen's clothing was ripped in a number of places and there were many scratches and cuts on his bruised face, arms and legs. Gorrin shook his head, tut-tutted and then removed his backpack and placed it on the floor. He quickly opened it and called for the healing ointment and a special potion. The air inside the pack seemed to swirl and then the ointment and a strange gold coloured glass bottle sparkled into view.

Michael anxiously spoke first, "Will he be alright, Gorrin?"

"Yes he will Michael, just as soon as I have had a chance to repair the damage, but I will have to work quickly to minimise the shock," replied Gorrin.

Richard had started to cry as soon as he had seen the battered state of Stephen. He was comforted by Michael, who gave him a brotherly hug as he said; "Don't worry Richard, our friend Gorrin says it will be okay, and I am sure he is right, after all, we know he can work magic don't we?"

Gorrin retrieved the items that had appeared in the top of the backpack and opened the stopper on the small glass bottle. Holding the bottle to Stephen's mouth, he moistened the injured boy's lips and these seemed to shimmer with golden sparkles as the liquid touched.

Stephen's eyes now flickered and he groaned in pain as his consciousness started to return. Gorrin put the bottle to Stephen's mouth again and whispered, "Drink this Stephen, it will help to make you well again." Stephen's mouth moved slightly as a little of the liquid ran on to his tongue and he coughed a little as the golden shimmering liquid reached the back of his mouth.

As Stephen began to take more and more of the strange liquid, a golden glow seemed to radiate from his skin and this got brighter and brighter until all the liquid in the small bottle had been drunk. As soon as the last drop had been drained from the bottle, Gorrin re-corked the stopper into the bottle and tapped it on the ground three times. The bottle sparkled gold and suddenly the bottle was full again. Gorrin then placed this into the backpack where it shimmered briefly before disappearing.

As the golden glow faded from Stephen's face, his original healthy colour started to return and his eyes opened fully. Meanwhile, Gorrin had carefully straightened Stephens damaged leg. The golden glow was still present in this particular leg as it was the most damaged part of Stephen and the glow concentrated on the area where the bones were broken.

Gorrin studied the leg critically for a few moments, then nodded and said: "Yes, that looks fine, but we need to sort out all of those scratches and cuts as well." He opened the tub of translucent gel and with a clean piece of wadding he had pulled from a pocket, he started to apply the salve to Stephens cuts and scratches. He passed the tub to Michael, together with more wadding and said, "Come on boys, you can both help," and so they all carefully applied the cream to the many cuts.

It wasn't long before Stephen was sitting up and all the many cuts, bruises and scratches had been repaired.

While they were sitting beside Stephen, waiting for the healing effects of the potion and the cream to fully take effect, Michael said, "Gorrin, um, I don't know how to say this but, well here goes – who are you and where are you from?" He looked directly at Gorrin as he asked the question and Richard did the same.

For a few seconds, Gorrin didn't answer as he was thinking deeply about the question. But, eventually Gorrin then started to tell the boys something of who he was and where he was from and when! Gorrin hadn't intended to say anything about his past, but the boys were all still obviously shocked and they needed something to take their minds of the very narrow escape that Stephen had managed, with help from Gorrin, of course. About ten minutes had passed when Stephen who by now had returned to alertness, said: "Thanks Gorrin. If it wasn't for you I'd be, well dead, I suppose."

Gorrin looked up sharply as he had been so engrossed with his story that he had not noticed Stephen's return to health, but he quickly recovered his composure and said, "Well my young friend, you are quite welcome, but you need to be more careful in future, I think the phrase is *Look before You Leap*!" And with that he chuckled, the boys joining in with relief, as much as from humour.

"Now then Stephen, can you stand?" asked Gorrin.

Stephen gingerly and a little shakily got to his feet, with support from his two brothers.

"Yes, very well done," Gorrin said, as he nodded his head with approval.

"What about all his ripped clothes though?" interrupted Michael.

Stephen looked down at his clothes and scowled and said, "I'm gonna be for it now."

Gorrrin shook his head and said, "No I have something else I can do about that."

Michael replied, "I was hoping you might have; only I didn't like to ask."

Pulling out of one of his tunic pockets, Gorrin produced a green velvet pouch and took a pinch of the powder out and sprinkled it over Stephen's clothes, singing a little song at the same time. The green sparkling powder covered the clothes which glittered green for a few seconds and suddenly they were clean and all damage had disappeared.

"Cool," said Michael, "I could really do with some of that dust, the number of times I get my clothes dirty, that would save me a telling off from my mum."

"Mmm," Gorrin replied, "But don't you think you should take better care of your clothes anyway?

"Well, yes I suppose," agreed Michael, rather grudgingly.

By now, it was virtually impossible to tell that Stephen had been badly hurt and all his clothing had been damaged, but, of course, with Gorrin's use of magic, all that had been reversed. The boys all now thanked Gorrin for helping them out with both finding Lucky their dog, as well as rescuing Stephen from the old cellar.

"Now boys," said Gorrin, "I want you to move a little further away, as I need to prevent anyone else from falling into the old cellar."

All three walked away from the site and turned to watch what Gorrin was going to do.

Gorrin pointed his runic staff at the old cellar and he started to sing in his ancient tongue.

The runes glowed green and a beam of green light shot from the end of the staff directly towards the cellar.

All the ground surrounding the cellar collapsed in a cloud of brick dust and soil. Gorrin kept the beam moving backwards and forwards across the area and the rubble continued to collapse until all cavities in the cellar had been filled. By the time Gorrin had finished with the green beam of light, all that remained of the dangerous cellar trap was a hollow in the ground. Gorrin had made sure that all brick and rubble had been turned into a coarse powder, but he was not yet finished.

Taking a large handful of the green repair powder out of the green velvet pouch he walked over to the hollow and scattered the powder over the ground, while he sang a little happy song. As soon as the powder hit the ground, it glittered with green stars and within seconds grass had started to grow. By the time Gorrin had finished the ground was safe to walk on and was completely covered with grass.

Smiling at his handiwork Gorrin walked over to the three boys, who had been watching the little man wield the powerful magic. The three boys ran over to meet Gorrin and thank him again for helping them. After much talk, Gorrin said that as the time was getting on, he needed to get back on the road again, and the boys needed to get home before it got dark.

All three boys were reluctant to leave Gorrin as they really liked the unusual and very likeable little man, but they understood the need to get home sooner, rather than later – particularly in the light of the afternoon's adventure.

Gorrin, made only one request, before they parted company, they mustn't mention Gorrin's use of magic

– but then who would believe them anyway? They shook hands enthusiastically before the boys with their dog headed off home. Gorrin stood for a few seconds watching them and then continued on in his original track southwards.

The gnome continued on for a couple more hours until the light was beginning to fade rapidly. He decided to stop and set up camp in the corner of a field with some hedging as shelter against the cold wind that was now beginning to bite. Gorrin sniffed the air and pursed his lips pensively. He could smell the onset of winter and he still had a fair few miles to go before getting to where his family were the last time he was visiting this part of the world.

Opening his backpack, he quickly retrieved the tent Brian had given him and it wasn't long before it was up and ready to sleep in. First he needed to make himself some hot food to keep out the chill that was now beginning to settle over the area. With his runic staff now illuminated like a torch, he gathered together a number of sticks and branches – enough to make a good fire. He extinguished his light and used his staff to light the fire.

As the red light struck the wood, it burst into flame and started to crackle. It wasn't long before Gorrin had a good blaze and his stew was bubbling merrily in the small aluminium Dixie along with another pot of water for his tea. A little while later, after he had finished eating his stew and was enjoying his hot sweet tea, he pulled out the sunstone and called for Brian. There was a brief pause and then the face of his friend swam into view on the surface of the smoky quartz stone's highly polished surface.

"Hello Brian, how are you my friend? " said Gorrin.

"Hi Gorrin, " replied Brian, "I'm fine, but how has your day gone?"

And so Gorrin proceeded to relate to Brian all about his adventure with the lost dog, and the problem with Stephen. It took about half an hour to recount the story and when he had finished Brian said, "Well Gorrin, you certainly seem to have a knack for finding trouble – or at least it seems to find you eh?"

"I suppose it does Brian, replied Gorrin, "But anyway, I had better get some sleep now as I have a long walk ahead of me tomorrow and I am quite tired after today's little escapade!"

"Well, I'm really not surprised Gorrin, but well, do try to keep things a bit lower key eh my old friend? Goodnight Gorrin." And with that the link was shutdown and Gorrin put the sunstone safely away.

Climbing into his sleeping bag that he had previously placed in the tent, he snuggled down for the night. To coin a phrase, he thought to himself, "Snug as a bug in a rug" and with that he went to sleep. His last thoughts as he slipped into sleep were that he must remember to write up his daily diary tomorrow and he resolved to do that first thing in the morning.

~~~~~~~~~~

Chapter Seventeen
"The motorcycle Gang"

Gorrin awoke to the sound of steady rain gently pattering on the tent fabric and as his consciousness returned; his thoughts went back to the events of the previous day. Opening his eyes he could see the grey light filtering through the tent material and the steam rising from his own breath. He was warm and snug in his sleeping bag cocoon and he was more than a little reticent about climbing out into the cold air.

He lay thinking for a little while, but eventually he reluctantly opened his sleeping bag and climbed out. The warm air from within the sleeping bag was released into the tent and the much cooler air reached Gorrin making him shiver. The air within the tent was actually warmer than the air outside the tent and it was not until he opened the tent flaps to peer out into the grey dreary wet morning that he realised this. He shivered again as the cold damp air wafted in through the open tent flaps.

 Looking across at the still smouldering remnants of the fire from the previous evening he decided that he needed to get the fire going if he was to have a hot drink to warm himself up.

By now the rain had almost stopped and there was just the faint hint of droplets of water in the air, so Gorrin decided to leave the tent to place more wood on to the fire. He climbed out through the tent flaps and stood up and looked around.

Now it was much lighter than it had been when he pitched camp the previous evening, he was now better able to see fuel for the fire. Only a few metres away from where he was camped lying under the bushes and trees, he spotted some old branches lying on the ground. He went over and picked them up grimacing slightly as his hands came into contact with the slightly slimy cold bark on the branch. "Urgh!" he said out loud. "That is rather unpleasant," he continued, "oh well it will have to do." He carried the wood over to where his fire lay smouldering.

Once he had piled sufficient wood on to the fire, he used his staff to give the fire the extra kick it needed to get it going properly. He paused briefly to look around to make sure that there was nobody in the vicinity and then used his magic. It was certainly easier than using his tinderbox or matches, he thought.

With the pot of water now placed into the small blaze, Gorrin retreated into the tent to get himself washed and dressed. He used a flannel to wash his face in a small bowl that he had called for from the backpack. He still had some drinking water with him, but he decided that at the next town, he would fill up the water containers. After all, he didn't want to risk running out.

Washing water was not a problem, as the rain coming down had partially filled one of his cooking pots that he had left outside, for just such a use. He chuckled to himself at his foresight in collecting the rainwater in a pot and started to hum a tune.

Soon he was washed and dressed and enjoying his morning tea, while he wrote up his diary in the journal that Brian had given him. It was certainly easier that using parchment and quill pen, he thought. His diary entry for the previous day complete, he went back outside and made his breakfast – he cooked himself some mushrooms and dried fruit from storage jars he carried in his backpack.

Once breakfast was finished, he quickly broke camp, making sure the sleeping bag, tent, pots and pans and other items were safely stowed away in his backpack. He used the green sparkling powder to repair the damage the fire had made and when he had finished, he surveyed the area. He nodded and gave a self-satisfied smile as he looked at the scene.

Apart from the grass that had been pressed down by the tent it was now almost impossible to tell that anyone had actually pitched a camp overnight. All chores now done, he slung the backpack on to his back, picked up the runic staff and started walking southwards again, humming a tune as he went.

As he walked the day started to brighten quite rapidly and it wasn't long before the first shards of blue sky could be seen peeping out between the grey of the rain clouds. He studied the sky as he walked and nodded to himself. "Yes," he thought, "the day has some promise at least, perhaps it may turn out to be better than I thought."

The day wore on and the morning passed quite quickly as the continued on his journey, still walking along but this time he had cut back through the hedgerow and was now walking alongside the roadway. A number of cars sped by, together with many lorries all heading southwards towards the village of Moreton-in-Marsh along the A44.

A few miles from the village he came to a fork in the road, he studied the large signpost carefully before making a decision to take the right hand road that was labelled A424 to Stow-on-the-Wold. He picked up his pace and got into a steady rhythm and started to hum again.

Looking around, there were still fields and trees, but the road that cut through it was far from peaceful. He was about three miles from the village, when a loud roaring noise approached him from behind along the road and moving at high speed. Gorrin quickly looked round, to see a large number of two wheeled machines, thundering along the road towards him.

As they shot past, he became aware that the helmeted and leather wearing riders were making loud whooping and jeering noises, though he was not sure at whom these were directed. It was not until the last of the eight riders had passed that it dawned on him that he was the target of these rather raucous catcalls. He frowned slightly at this thought and turned on his heel looking at the rapidly disappearing backs of the motorcyclists as they headed towards the village.

About an hour later he was approaching the outskirts of the village and he noticed that the traffic was slowing as it passed him. His sharp eyesight had already spotted the motorcyclists lined up in a side road. Three of the riders were still astride their machines, but the other five were standing talking to two other figures.

Gorrin looked closely at what was happening and realised that the conversation underway between the motorcyclists and the other two was not friendly. Indeed, the tone of the voices as he strained to hear above the noise of the traffic from the fraction he could hear, was definitely the opposite.

The motorcyclists did not see Gorrin approach, as they were too intent on the two persons they had surrounded. Gorrin could see from the wary faces of the two that they were teenagers aged about seventeen. Gorrin made a rapid decision, as he did not like the look at what appeared to be developing with the gang of motorcyclists. Gorrin hid behind a nearby stonewall and rubbed the amethyst stone on his ring, singing the ancient charm song at the same time. He shimmered for a couple of seconds and faded rapidly from view until he was completely invisible.

Gorrin stood up and moved closer to where the motorcyclist gang was, to better hear what was happening and to observe more closely. At this point he was not about to interfere, after all, he had promised Brian that he would do his best not to get involved and use his magic in public.

"You owe us," said the dark haired and tallest motorcyclist, to the male youth now standing in the middle of the leather clad group. The boy was plainly scared of the group as Gorrin could see his eyes darting left and right along the group. In spite of this, he answered back but in a pleading voice saying, "Look, Tony, I don't have the money, I only have a couple of quid."

"Well John, that will do for starters, but if you ain't got the dosh, then we'll have to take it out of your hide, eh mates?" As Tony said this, he looked around the group for the support he knew would be forthcoming.

At this news, the youth grabbed the hand of his girlfriend and they dodged through the group and headed off down the country lane. The speed and suddenness of their departure caught the motorcyclists off guard and for a few seconds they just paused as if digesting the sight of their prey's rapid exit. Then with a nasty shout to his gang, Tony shouted, "Come on let's get em." And with that, those on foot ran for their motorbikes and started their engines. As they roared into life, the noise was deafening and the bikers started to give chase to the two retreating figures.

Gorrin had heard enough to know that these bikers were up to no good and needed to be taught a lesson. As this thought crossed his mind, he briefly considered whether he should stay out of this, but he was not about to let a lot of bullies beat up the two figures running up the lane.

He pointed his staff at the last of the bikes and started to sing an ancient charm and the runes on the staff started to glow red. A split second later a red beam shot out of the end of the staff towards the rear wheel of the back most motorcycle. Instantly the tyre melted and exploded with a large "Bang!"

Gorrin quickly moved the beam across to the second machine and the rear tyre also melted and went "Bang!"

Both machines started to wobble all over the place and came to an abrupt halt as their riders realised that something serious was amiss with their motorcycles. The riders turned to look stupidly at their, now flat rear tyres, but were unaware of Gorrin, who was still invisible.

The other six bikers had already moved off. Their riders, while they were aware of the two bangs, they had not understood what had caused them or what the consequences of them were. It was not long before they had caught up with the two figures they were chasing.

John turned to face the gang and shouted, "Run for it Jayne."

Jayne turned to John and shook her head shouting back as she did so, "I won't leave you to these cowards."

The six remaining gang members ran towards the two and tried to grab hold of them but both John and Jayne resisted and tried to punch and kick them back. At first the two were successful in repelling them, but the force of numbers was beginning to tell and they were both beginning to tire quickly.

Gorrin meanwhile had decided to follow, but the distance that the remaining six motorcyclists had travelled, was much too far for Gorrin to follow quickly enough. He decided to use magic to cover the distance, so he produced the purple velvet pouch and took a small pinch and dusted himself with the strangely glittering powder. Reciting the song there was a "Pop!" sound and Gorrin vanished completely, to reappear close to where the bikers had stopped and were now busily attacking the two.

Gorrin looked at the scene that greeted his arrival with great dismay, for the two, whom he had seen run off, were now fighting the bikers, but were losing. John had succeeded in knocking one of the assailants to the ground and the individual was laying on the ground moaning. Just as two managed to grab hold of John to allow the others to punch him, Gorrin intervened.

Gorrin deplored the use of force under normal circumstances, but there were times in his life when he has used it. It was always his last resort, and this was one of those times he decided.

Gorrin was still invisible and this was a major advantage. He advanced holding his runic staff, his blue eyes blazing at the sight of the conflict in front of him, and he started to whirl the staff around.

Something that Gorrin had not spoken about before to his friend Brian, was that he was fully trained in Gnomish martial arts. This included the use of the runic staff as a fighting weapon, as well as the art of various forms of unarmed combat. Unfortunately for Gorrin, it had been many centuries since he had last had to use them, so his skills were more than a little rusty.

The result of the lack of practice, was that the runic staff flew from his hand and slammed into the middle of the back of one of the bikers. The effect was immediate – the biker dropped to his knees and fell forward to roll around on the ground, clutching his back. Gorrin had run towards the struggling group to pick up the staff before someone else did.

The bikers, who had been punching or holding the two, looked around to see who had attacked one of their number, but there was no one to be seen, except for a strangely carved stick that seemed to have appeared from nowhere.

The biker, closest to the one who had been hit in the back with the staff, made a grab for the runic staff, but just as his fingers closed around the end of the stick, it seemed to take on a life of its own. What the biker had not realised, because he could not seen him, was that Gorrin had just reached the runic staff also and had just managed to grab hold of the end of the staff at the same time that the biker had.

All that the other bikers could see was that the stick suddenly started to fade from view, as did the arm of the biker and, in his surprise at this strange effect the biker had immediately let go of the stick. As soon as he let go, the biker's arm had shimmered back into view, but the look of astonishment on his face, indicated to Gorrin that he was momentarily caught off-guard.

This was enough for him to use the stick to sweep the biker's legs from under him and he hit the ground with a dull thud and gasped as the air was knocked out of him.

Gorrin started to sing a song and pointed the staff at the now winded biker and the runes on the staff started to glow a pink colour. A pink light shot out of the end of the staff and struck the biker full in the chest. Again, surprise was evident on the biker's face – just before he went to sleep.

Some of the bikers had seen these strange events and when the pink light materialised out of thin air to strike one of their gang and knock him out cold, two of them started to panic and head back for their motorcycles. That left the one fighting John and the two trying to hold Jayne. The distraction was all that Jayne needed, and she caught one of the attackers with a high kick in the side – he dropped like a sack of old potatoes to the ground.

John was now lying cut and battered on the ground from the pounding the largest of the bikers had given him and who was standing over him about to give him a good kicking. But John was not completely spent, for he managed to kick out and catch Tony, the large biker and the gang leader, on the shin and that was enough to over balance him. As he fell back, the strange and ghostly pink light came into existence again to hit him full in the back. He stood motionless for a few seconds as his eyes glazed over, and then he fell forward to sprawl across the grass.

Gorrin had not been idle, since as soon as he had put the first to sleep, he had turned his attention to another target. He saw John get knocked to the ground and the larger biker standing over him about to kick the youth on the ground, when John had managed to kick him in the shin. This was sufficient time for Gorrin to move forward and fire his staff again at the larger biker and it had caught the large man straight in the back.

Jayne took advantage of this distraction to twist out of the biker's grip, but the biker was not about to let go of his prey. As he tried to hold on, Jayne caught him with a kick straight in the stomach and the biker folded up and hit the ground. Turning, she ran over to where John was lying to help him stand, all the while looking around to see if the strange pink light was about to appear again.

While Jayne had gone over to see if John was alright, the biker she had just kicked, had managed to recover and was standing up with a view to attacking her from behind, but just as he started to run at her the strange pink light appeared again and struck him full on the chest.

He just sighed and slumped to the floor as if in slow motion, to lie motionless, except for the fact that he was snoring his head off.

Jayne had heard the movement behind her and as her head had spun round, she had seen the flash of a pink beam of light shoot past her head. Her eyes widened as the potential attacker had just sort of conked out. She turned around to see where the light had come from. Like someone appearing out of mist, she saw a short figure materialise out of the thin air.

Standing before her, dressed in green and carrying a backpack, holding what appeared to be some sort of walking stick was a very short man. What particularly caught her attention, apart from the obvious fact that this man had just appeared, were the stranger's very bright blue eyes.

"Hello," said the small figure. "My name is Gorrin, what are your names?"

~~~~~~~~~~~~~~~~

Chapter Eighteen
"Motorcycles and magic"

For a few seconds Jayne did not say anything. The moment was broken by the groans of John as he tried to rise from the ground. Jayne turned to look at John and moved over to where he was sitting. Gorrin had also moved over to where John was and he put out his hand to help John get to his feet.

John rather unsteadily stood up, supported by Gorrin and Jayne and looked at Gorrin. He had seen this short man appear out of thin air, after the amazing light show that that literally stunned their assailants. John answered Gorrin's enquiry. "Thanks for your help Mr Gorrin. I'm John and this is Jayne."

"I'm pleased to meet you both, and please just call me Gorrin, as that is my first name. I don't normally give out any other names, as names can have a power of their own," Gorrin replied a little cryptically. "Now then, where do you hurt John and Jayne, and while I am looking after that, perhaps you can tell me why this gang of ruffians took it upon themselves to try to beat you into a pulp?"

While Gorrin rummaged in his backpack for his healing ointment, Jayne started to tell Gorrin their story. The gang were well known in the area and had been busily terrorising people in the area. The police knew them, but as everyone was too scared to talk about the threats and damage, as well as the extortion of money, no action had yet been taken against the gang.

As Gorrin applied the salve to John and Jayne's bruises and cuts, he listened intently to the story, frowning as the story unrolled. It finally came to the part where Gorrin had arrived at the scene, and the gang were threatening to beat up John if he didn't pay them 'protection' money.

The cream rapidly did its magical work and soon all the cuts and bruises had vanished as though they had never existed. Jayne looked on with astonishment at the incredible way the bruises and cuts seemed to shimmer slightly and then simply fade away. This short man carried some amazing things – she wondered if he was some sort of extra-terrestrial, but that notion seemed to be too far fetched. John meanwhile, continued with the story.

The gang leader had said that John's family might have a 'run of bad luck' if he did not pay up. When it became obvious to John and Jayne that they were likely to be attacked anyway, as they did not have enough money to pay them, they had then tried to escape – but, of course, the gang had caught up with them. It was only the intervention of Gorrin that had saved them from being more seriously hurt.

Gorrin looked around at the sleeping figures of the remaining gang and came to a decision. He would have to intervene further, otherwise John and Jayne were likely to be beaten up later when the gang awoke. He looked into his backpack again and called for his magic grimoire. The book shimmered into view at the top of the pack and again the two were astonished.

The book was covered with black leather and had golden runic writing stencilled across the front of the cover. There was a golden lock that fastened the book to prevent opening and this was firmly holding the book, stopping any unauthorised opening of the ancient tome.

As Jayne and John looked on at the scene of Gorrin and the backpack, they could see that the surface of the bookbinding appeared to glisten in the daylight, as if the book itself was wet. The edges of the pages that they could see were covered in gold leaf. Gorrin sang to the book in an almost strident tone. The apparent wetness of the book faded from view as the song hung in the air.

Gorrin then used his ring with its inset amethyst to open the lock. As the lock fell away from the book, Gorrin sang to the book for a second time, but this time the song was more of a caress. Gorrin opened the book and the pages that had been blank seemed to become misty. As the song continued, the writing that lay concealed on the pages by magic swam into view.

While Gorrin was singing his song, Jayne had continued to think about what she had witnessed so far and came to the conclusion that this was not advanced technology from an extra-terrestrial, but was some sort of magic. She decided to say something to Gorrin.

"You are using magic aren't you Gorrin?" enquired Jayne.

Gorrin stopped singing and looked across at Jayne and said, "You are quite perceptive my young friend. Yes it is indeed magic. A very ancient magic, and if I am not mistaken, it is the like of which you have never seen before?"

Jayne grew excited at this news, but Gorrin waved her silent, saying "I need to deal with these 'sleeping beauties' before they awake, as that spell wont keep them out for too long and we don't want to take any chances now do we?"

Jayne fell silent at this request and looked around to make sure that the gang members were still asleep. Satisfied that all was still okay, she looked back at Gorrin. She saw that he was thumbing through the pages carefully studying their contents. She continued to study him, when Gorrin paused to look at a particular page for a few seconds. His lips moved in silence as he recited the spell from the page. Sure that he had the spell memorised, he moved on through the book until he found the second spell that he was looking for.

Now that Gorrin was sure that he had the appropriate spells, he closed the book and fastened the lock and replaced the book into his backpack. He picked the pack back up and shouldered it on to his back and then pointing the runic staff at the nearest of the sleeping bikers, he recited the first spell, and then followed this quickly with the second spell.

The runic lettering on the staff glowed faintly as he recited the memorised enchantments. Gorrin quickly moved on to the next biker and the process was repeated, until all of the sleeping bikers had been bound by the two spells.

That task completed, Gorrin moved to where John and Jayne were and said. "I think it will be best if you move behind those trees out of direct sight, as I don't want to confuse them anymore that they are going to be."

John and Jayne both nodded and walked over to the adjacent trees and hid behind in a position to be able to watch, but not interfere.

The sleeping bikers all started to awake and as they opened their eyes they were obviously in a trance-like state. Gorrin then whispered into the ears of each one in turn and then using the ring, made himself invisible. Gorrin's sudden disappearance alarmed Jayne and John, but they became even more startled when he reappeared close to where they were hiding.

John exclaimed, "How did you do that?"

"Hush!" hissed Gorrin. "Keep quiet, I don't want to confuse those troublemakers anymore than they are already."

Meanwhile, the remaining motorcyclists had climbed back on to their bikes, started them and ridden off back into town. Once they had disappeared into the distance, Jayne asked a question, "Whatever did you say and do to them, Gorrin?"

"Oh!" said Gorrin innocently, but with a mischievous glint in his eyes, "I just suggested that they should take themselves down to the nearest police station and confess all of their wrong doings. In fact, I have actually made it so that they will have to tell the truth to any questions put to them."

John and Jayne both looked at each other at this news, then back at Gorrin and they laughed. Then they said together: "But what about the others, won't they still come after us?"

"They might," said Gorrin in reply, "But I think they will be too busy trying to evade the police, as their friends will have made sure that they were implicated also, I don't think that they'll be giving you any trouble anytime soon. I wouldn't be surprised if they are not in prison for some time at least – and they won't have a clue as to why they confessed in the first place."

At this news, John and Jayne let out a laugh, but this was more of relief than satisfaction. Gorrin joined in the laughter, but his was more tempered by feelings that he was doing his best to hide.

Gorrin, who had been engrossed with the events just enacted, had been steadily growing a little anxious, as if someone was watching. He had even taken the trouble to look around, although in such a way as to be discreet. He could not see anyone, but this nagging feeling of being watched would not go away and it was making him feel more than a little uncomfortable. It was a feeling that he had not felt for a very long time.

As the laughter subsided, John asked a direct question, "Look Gorrin, It's obvious that you know a lot about magic, in fact I have always believed that magic didn't exist, and was only a lot of stories made up by superstitious people, to explain things they didn't have a clue about."

"Well, you are partly right," replied Gorrin. "People in the past did make up a lot of stories about magic, but they did have more than a grain of truth in them. Magic does exist and for good or ill, but that depends on the user. If magic is used for good, then it is termed white or light magic and if used for ill, then it is dark or black magic. The problem is that there is generally a rule of three."

"What do you mean a rule of three?" enquired Jayne quickly.

Gorrin paused briefly before replying, "Well, if you inflict harm on someone for personal gain, then you get the harm back, one way or another, three-fold. Likewise, if you perform good with it, then the good luck that returns is three-fold the amount you have given."

Jayne paused before saying, "I see, but surely what you just did is personal gain?"

"No," said Gorrin, "More a case of natural justice, after all, they have all been causing more than a little mischief in these parts, for some considerable time, have they not?"

He finished with a question, but of course he already knew the answer, he was just trying to get the point across to Jayne.

"There is one point, however," continued Gorrin. "I am not supposed to interfere with human affairs, but I have always interpreted that to mean on a much larger scale."

Jayne responded to this statement saying, "Aren't you treading a fine line with that Gorrin?"

"Sometimes" replied Gorrin, somewhat cryptically.

There was a slight pause as Jayne and John digested this information. Gorrin grew a little uncomfortable at the silence and asked a question. "Er, I would rather that no one else gets to hear about this little event, if you see what I mean. "

"Of course," replied both Jayne and John. "But then again, who would believe us in any case!"

Jayne continued; "But what about the bikers? Won't they remember?"

"No" replied Gorrin, "I made them forget that part as well."

A few more seconds passed while Jayne and John thought about what Gorrin had just told them, until finally Jayne said: "Now, where exactly are you from then Gorrin? I'm sure that is a story worth telling."

Gorrin, who had lapsed into deep thought at this point, looked up at that and his face brightened, Well yes I think I can tell you at least some of my past history, but first I would really like a nice cup of hot sweet tea."

Jayne and John looked at each other and then back at Gorrin and they both exclaimed together, "Of course, there is a tea room close by."

"Sounds good to me," said Gorrin. And with that the three headed back into the village towards the nearest tea room.

It wasn't long before all three were sat down at a table with a large pot of tea and two cappuccino coffees. Gorrin had never seen such drinks before and he asked if he could try a sip of one. Jayne chuckled at this and obliged by passing him her cup. As he carefully raised the cup to his lips, he could smell the milky aroma of coffee and his nose twitched at this new and delicious smelling aroma.

After tasting the coffee, he returned to his pot of tea. While he found the taste of the coffee was very rich and tasty, he still preferred hot sweet tea – although he was quite sure that he would be drinking such coffees in the future.

Gorrin started to explain to Jayne and John at least some of his recent adventures, as well as a very brief explanation about his life, prior to his accident with the sleep that had resulted in his spending over three hundred and fifty years in a form of hibernation.

When he had finished his story, Jayne and John were both silent for a moment as they were too astonished. This story was the stuff of fiction – or so they had thought up until that point. And, if they hadn't actually seen the magic used, they would have said that this rather unusual little man was either 'off his head' or was just lying his head off.

Gorrin looked down into his tea and thought about his family again. He needed to try to dowse for them again. He cleared a small space and pulled out his map and the special dowsing crystal, along with a small silver brooch that belonged to his mother. Holding the silver chain that was attached to the crystal, with the brooch clutched in the palm of his hand, he held it over the map that showed the south of the Oxford area. The crystal rotated on its chain, but there was no strong indication that there was anyone from his family there.

Jayne and John had been watching Gorrin intently, and Jayne had realised what Gorrin was doing. John, however, had not the slightest idea what was taking place, and he looked quizzically across at Jayne. Jayne saw the expression on John's face and realised that he did not understand. She silently mouthed the word 'dowsing', but John didn't understand, so she repeated, but to no avail.

Gorrin looked up at this and saw the silent conversation and smiled and said, "I'm dowsing John." John was still no clearer and said: "Why are you looking for water Gorrin?"

"Oh you idiot John!" exclaimed Jayne, "Gorrin's not looking for water; he is looking for his family."

Gorrin nodded to confirm this, chuckling also, "Jayne's quite right John, I am not looking for water, although it is possible to do that. In fact, I am looking for any sign that my family might be in the area, but I haven't had any luck so far."

John felt a little sheepish at his lack of understanding and said, "Well how was I to know and anyway, how is it that you seem to know so much?" John's query was directed at Jayne and she answered, "Oh, I suppose I must have read or seen it somewhere."

Having drawn a blank with the dowsing, Gorrin carefully put the brooch and crystal back into his pocket and folded up the map. He looked up at his two new friends and said, "I'm afraid I must go now as I have to get on with my journey."

Jayne and John were both a little sad at this news, as they had both quickly gotten to like this unusual little man with his white hair and twinkling blue eyes. But, of course, they both realised that he had to continue his quest, if he was to discover what had happened to his family.

Gorrin stood up and shook hands with John, while Jayne gave him a big hug and a kiss – this was quite a surprise to Gorrin and he blushed at this familiarity, as he wasn't used to it.

Wishing them all the very best and promising to pop in next time he was back this way, Gorrin left the pair at the table and went out through the doorway into the street, to continue on his journey southwards again.

As Gorrin continued along the road, towards Burford he still had the distinct impression that he was being followed. He looked around but there was no one in sight.

"This was strange," he thought to himself, "It's not like me to be getting nervous."

Just as he thought this, a voice he hadn't heard in a long time, came out of thin air, just behind him.

"Still trying to solve the problems of humans then Gorrin, don't you ever learn?"

Gorrin recognised that voice from the past and a shiver ran down his spine at the thought. He turned around and said: "Hello Horrin!"

~~~~~~~~~~~~~~~

Chapter Nineteen
"Horrin"

For a few seconds, there was no reply. The sound of the wind through the trees was all that could be heard. Then about two metres behind where Gorrin was standing, the air started to shimmer as if in a heat haze. A small figure, dressed in a black jacket and black trousers, with black boots, appeared out of the thin air.

The small man had a grey beard and grey hair and his eyes were the same shade of startling blue as Gorrin's and he was holding a runic staff. The runic staff looked identical to Gorrin's, except that it appeared to be much darker in colour. What caught Gorrin's eye was the way the wood itself seemed to swirl like a dark mist.

"Well, well, well, so you did know it was me following you then?" enquired Horrin.

"Not at first I didn't, but I began to suspect though, after I had come out of the tea room." replied Gorrin. "There was something familiar about that feeling – it was one I hadn't felt in a long, long time."

"So where have you been then Gorrin?" Horrin asked, but there was a malicious edge to his voice, and Gorrin picked up on that straight away.

Gorrin stared hard at the other gnome and his eyes narrowed slightly as a thought occurred to him. "You wouldn't happen to know something about that would you?" said Gorrin.

"Perhaps," replied Horrin, a little evasively. Horrin stared back at Gorrin with an impassive look. He wanted to continue this little game, as he was enjoying the look on Gorrin's face.

Meanwhile, Gorrin's thoughts had been racing and he rapidly thought back to the time when he had set the charm on himself, all those years ago. Try as he might, he could not see where he had made a mistake with his magic, but then, there was no such thing as a perfect spell and things could always go wrong, in the most unexpected ways sometimes. He had set a protection charm in place on his home to protect it from view and from anyone who could mean him harm – or so he had thought. His thoughts returned to the present as Horrin spoke again.

"Still trying to work it out eh? Well maybe I'll put you out of your misery and maybe I wont. That all depends," finished Horrin.

"Depends on what?" queried Gorrin.

"On you, of course," replied Horrin. "Where are you heading then, my old friend?" continued Horrin.

"As if you didn't know," retorted Gorrin. "Anyway, stop getting off the point."

He paused for a few seconds as his thought processes continued, then he said, "It was you wasn't it."

"Me?" replied Horrin in mock surprise, "Whatever do you mean?"

"You know very well what I am talking about Horrin. It was you who tampered with my sleeping charm," said Gorrin accusingly.

"Well yes and no," replied Horrin. "I wasn't actually there, as you well know, and your protection spell you put over your home was very good." He paused for a few seconds, to let Gorrin digest this information and also to enjoy the discomfort that was now evident on Gorrin's face.

Then he continued, "And while you were out, before you returned, I managed to get in and leave you a little present." As he finished with this revelation, he started to laugh, and then said. "I never dreamed that it would have had such a great effect."

Gorrin was not in the least amused, but it explained how his charm had gone so badly wrong. There was, however, a side effect to the spell that Horrin had not counted on. During the three hundred and fifty years, Gorrin had not aged one little bit. This was a fact that Horrin had also picked up on as he studied the other.

"I thought we had managed to deal with you, after that episode with the bubonic plague in 1649. " Gorrin continued: "You seem to have reclaimed your staff I see."

"Yes and no thanks to your meddling," replied Horrin. It was his turn to frown now and his eyes glared dangerously as his mind went back to that time long ago. In spite of the intervening years it was obvious to Gorrin that he had hit on a raw nerve.

"I had quite a good thing going, with all that chaos I caused," said Horrin darkly.

"The power I was wielding was quite intoxicating. But then you had to interfere – you and that damn *Gnome Code.*"

Gorrin looked closely at Horrin before he replied. He was watching the other gnome's hands and checking to see if this renegade gnome was about to hurl any magic in his direction. Satisfied that he was safe – at least for the moment, he continued the conversation. "It was not before time I think. You made quite an impact on things, one way or another and we just had to stop you. And stop you, we did, although it took a lot to try to repair all the damage that you did. And you managed to vaporise two of my friends in the process, before we subdued you."

At this point, Horrin's eyes flashed dangerously in Gorrin's direction and he responded verbally in a hissing tone; "Yes, and then you placed me in stasis. But that didn't manage to hold me very long as you can see, I broke free of the crystal."

Gorrin's curiosity came to the fore at this point, as he asked, "Just how did you break free of that then?"

It was Horrin's turn to pause and look thoughtful. His mind went back to the time he had spent encased in that crystal, with only his thoughts to keep himself company. But while he was trapped, he had consoled himself with the knowledge that he had left a booby trap in his arch-enemy's own home.

More than a hundred years had passed, while he had also pondered his fate entrapped within the crystal. Fortunately for Horrin, the magic that had trapped him had started to weaken with time and his own powers had been strong enough to break the enchantment. His efforts to break free, however, had severely weakened him and by the time the crystal had disintegrated in a shower of tiny splinters, he had needed to hide from those who had entrapped him as punishment.

Horrin answered Gorrin's question with a question of his own, "Before I answer, how did you manage to escape my little present?"

Gorrin replied: "The magic had started to fail and I was woken up by my house falling down about my ears!"

"Oh good, well at least it was nothing serious then!" retorted Horrin sarcastically. "Anyway, how is it that you haven't aged? That is one trick I would like to know."

Now it was Gorrin's turn to look thoughtful, but quickly he replied, "I have not the slightest idea, but it is, no thanks to you, of that I have no doubt."

"Ha!" said Horrin, "Knowing how you always keep messing up the magic, it's a wonder you never managed to blow yourself up."

As this was more than a little close to the mark, Gorrin could not help but blush at this comment. Horrin, of course, picked up on that immediately.

"Oh, so I'm right on target then I see," Horrin mocked.

Gorrin was about to respond when he changed his tack by saying, "Well at least I don't blow up my own kind, unlike you! I thought the humans were warlike enough, until you came on the scene, then, of course, they didn't know what had hit them."

Horrin grimaced at this comment, and through gritted teeth, replied, "They should not have got in my way!"

Immediately Gorrin retorted: "You didn't give them a chance to get away, you just used your staff and blew them away!"

Horrin did not like the way this conversation was going and was becoming increasingly angered by Gorrin. As his anger built up, his fingers tightened on the runic staff. Gorrin was watching very closely and had seen a slight change in the finger pressure that Horrin was exerting on the staff. Gorrin prepared to protect himself and started to hum a protection charm.

Horrin did not notice at first, as he was still thinking of a suitable reply to Gorrin's scathing remarks. Then the sound was picked up by his sharp hearing and he stared fixedly at Gorrin for a few seconds, before saying: " You need not worry Gorrin, I have no intention of harming you – at least not yet," he added menacingly.

Gorrin stopped humming, but warily studied the other, then said: "So just why have you decided to pay me a visit then?"

"Oh, I had heard that you were looking for your long lost family," answered Horrin.

"Just what do you know of my family Horrin!" Gorrin's eyes blazed dangerously as he spoke. This sudden strength of purpose in his voice caused Horrin to step back slightly, ready to ward himself against anything Gorrin might decide to do.

There was another pause, while Horrin deliberated what to say. The momentary pause caused Gorrin to question Horrin again, "Well, answer my question Horrin, what do you know about my family?"

"I know that they aren't where you think they are," he answered evasively.

Gorrin hoped that this information meant that they still alive, but beyond that the information was useless.

"So where are they then? You seem to have all the answers after all." Gorrin continued, "Well, come on then, tell me what you know?"

Horrin deliberated for a few more seconds and then came to a decision.

"You will just have to find them, with no help from me – they mean less than nothing to me in any case! Till we meet again Gorrin!" And with that Horrin slammed the end of the runic staff into the ground and in a split second Horrin appeared to be shrouded in what could only be described as 'black light', and then he was gone, leaving only faint ripples in the air that rapidly faded away.

Gorrin let out a gasp of air with the relief that the encounter was over, but just to make sure he hummed a song and moved his staff around to check for a hidden presence. As the staff did not vibrate, it meant that there was no one magically concealed nearby, so Gorrin ceased singing. During the meeting with Horrin, he had not noticed that the sounds around had seemed to fade away. Only now was he aware of the everyday noises of the wind in the trees and the sound of the evening bird chorus as the birds retired for the night.

He became conscious that the light was beginning to fade. This particular day seemed to have been more eventful that most, but had passed so quickly he had not noticed the time passing. He turned on his heel and started to walk southwards again with a purposeful stride.

After about half an hour had passed, it became very apparent that the light was now almost gone. He found a suitable place just the other side of a hedgerow and set up camp, using his staff as a torch. It wasn't long before he was busily cooking a tin of thick vegetable soup over a nice warming fire. As the soup heated on the fire, his thoughts ran back over his meeting with Horrin. Gorrin's thoughts were broken by the soup bubbling over the side and into the fire, to hiss and spit angrily back at him. He looked up and carefully lifted the pan off the fire and poured the contents into a dish to eat.

The meal was soon finished and he sat down to write up the events of the day. This took him longer than usual, as his mind kept wandering off to think about Horrin and what he had said. It wasn't a case of what he had said, however, more a case of the way he had said it. There was obviously a lot that Gorrin did not know about his family, but there was nothing he could do about that, except to continue to search for them.

He tried again with the sunstones and again with the map and crystal, but both methods did not result in any success. After he had put his things away, he decided to set up a protection spell around his camp, just in case his visitor returned. Once his camp was secure, he settled down in his sleeping bag and drifted off to fitful sleep.

He awoke early, before it was light and made himself breakfast. Soon he had cleared his campsite and was back on the road again. He walked a number of miles, but his impatience was now beginning to get the better of him. He decided that he was going to use magic to travel. This was a decision that he did not take lightly, but the appearance of Horrin had changed things considerably. Now, more than ever, he needed to find his family and find out what had happened in the intervening years.

Gorrin felt in his jacket pocket and pulled out the purple pouch that contained the teleportation powder. He took a pinch out of the pouch and sprinkled the strangely glittering powder on his clothes, while singing the incantation. There was a 'pop' and Gorrin disappeared. As the road was reasonably straight and he had a good view, he managed to travel several miles at a time.

This method of transport was more than a little tricky. Sometimes he materialised just above the grass verge at the side of the road, to land in a small heap. Other times, he would appear within brambles, which was really quite painful. Once he managed to land in the drainage ditch at the side of the road.

It was not long before he had covered the distance to Burford and then on to Lechlade. He was still travelling through the Cotswolds and this was a part of the country that had not altered greatly in the last few hundred years – except, of course for the road itself and the traffic that was now heading along it.

While he was in Lechlade, he noticed that there was a vehicle that was picking up passengers and he remembered that Brian had called this transport a bus. He decided that he would give it a try, as he was getting more than a little sick and tired of landing in cow pats and drainage ditches. As he climbed on to the bus and handed over the money for the fare, he noticed that some of the other passengers eyed him curiously and their noses wrinkled as the odour of cow dung reached them.

The bus continued its journey eastwards, towards Wantage and Gorrin nodded off to sleep. Gorrin was finally awoken, by the jolting of the bus, as it came to a halt in Abingdon. He climbed out and looked around and recognised little of the area as so much had changed in the past few centuries.

He looked at the map and worked out where he was. It was with a great shock that he finally realised what it was that Horrin had been cryptically referring to. His family's home had been demolished to make way for a large new road. Stunned he sat down by the side of the road. "Where was he to go now?" he thought.

He pulled out his map again and tried to dowse with the crystal. Of course, there was no reaction in this area, so he carefully moved the rotating crystal to the most southern part of the map. He almost missed it, but a very slight clockwise movement just caught his attention.

He focused his thoughts and stared at the map and crystal. Yes. There was definitely a slight movement of the glittering stone. His face brightened at this apparent good news. The movement was only faint, but it was enough to give him hope. He decided he needed another map, but one that covered the area further south. He had noticed that there was a large bookshop on the high street, so he headed to it and went inside. After asking several of the sales staff, he eventually found what he was looking for and quickly paid for it and left the shop, with the map clutched tightly in his hand.

He found a quiet area where there was a bench and opened the map and placed it on to the wooden seat. With the crystal and chain firmly held in his hand he started to dowse again. He moved the rotating crystal across the map and the stone on its chain started to rotate faster and faster, until he focused on an area of forest that lay close to a small village in the New Forest.

As Gorrin stared at the map, he let out an exclamation full of emotion. "Of course, why didn't I think of that sooner? That's where they are – they are in the New Forest!"

Recklessly he pulled out of his pocket his purple pouch again and dusted his clothes with a good couple of pinches of the powder. There was a loud 'POP!' and Gorrin disappeared from view. As he vanished, two fifteen-year-old schoolboys who were playing truant from school, saw the sight. The sudden disappearance of this odd looking stranger, right in front of them, sent them off in a wild panic. They were still gabbling on about it, several hours later, but nobody believed them and everyone thought that they had been drinking.

Meanwhile, Gorrin had re-appeared many, many miles from where he had vanished and he was now clinging rather precariously to the uppermost branches of a tree, and the branch on which he was standing had just started to make an ominous cracking sound.

~~~~~~~~

Chapter Twenty
"Reunion in Ashurst"

Gorrin clung precariously to his perch high up in the oak tree, with all thoughts of his encounter with Horrin pushed out of his mind. He looked around quickly to take in his predicament. Obviously, he had made a serious mistake and now he was going to have to get himself out of this mess, before he hurt himself.

As he struggled to maintain his grip on the branches, there was a loud 'crack'! For a split second he was suspended in mid-air and then he started to fall as the branch had just given way.

Down went Gorrin and as he started his earthwards plunge he scrabbled wildly for a means to slow his rapid descent to the ground. It was fortunate that gnomes are very solidly built, as he bounced off various branches on his way down. Branches and the remains of a few leaves whipped past his head, and he suffered scratches to his face and hands on the way down.

Gorrin was no more than four metres from the ground, when he managed to grab hold of a strong enough branch and prevent himself from falling any further. The strain on his arms as his full weight was taken up, made him feel that his arms were being pulled out of their sockets. As he had grabbed hold of the branch, the runic staff which he had been holding, was released and it continued its downward plunge to land in a pile of horse dung at the base of the oak tree.

Gorrin's arms were now starting to get tired, as he had not managed to get a proper foothold on any near branches. He was hanging from the branch, rather like washing hanging from the clothes line and this odd comparison ran briefly through his mind – just before he decided that the only thing to do was to let go and hopefully drop to the ground unharmed.

Readying himself for the impact with the ground he let go of the branch and continued his descent. Splat! Gorrin had hit the ground on his feet, but the grass was obviously used by the New Forest ponies and horses and was covered in their dung and so he immediately slipped straight on to his back, right in the middle of the pile.

Winded from the fall he just lay there for a few seconds, trying to gather his thoughts together, while he stared up at the tree from which he had just fallen. He slowly sat up and realised that he had quite a number of bruises, cuts and scratches, not to mention the very strong smell that was now reaching his nose. "Oh well", he thought. "At least it was a soft landing!"

He slowly and carefully stood up, as the ground was very slippery. Looking around he noticed that his runic staff was sticking out of another pile a couple of metres away. He walked over to it and pulled it out of the ground, pulling a face and wrinkling his nose as he realised that the top of the staff where it was normally held, was the end that had been embedded in the unpleasant material.

He found a suitable place to wipe it on clean grass and then thought about his own somewhat dirty condition. Looking down at his clothes he saw that he was in a very messy state and needed to clean himself up. "Well," he thought, "he was going to have to use some more magic to do that, but since there was no one around, it wouldn't matter."

Gorrin felt in his jacket pocket and pulled out the green velvet pouch then opened it. He took a large pinch of green powder from the pouch and threw it up into the air and started to sing in his ancient tongue, the charm that mended, cleaned and repaired things. The dust glittered green, then white and all the horse dung and dirt that was clinging to him shimmered and disappeared.

Looking at his handiwork, he nodded and smiled and looked back up at the top of the tree from where he had so recently fallen. He was very lucky, he thought, not to have broken an arm or a leg and he winced as he felt the soreness of the scratches and bruises. He really needed to stop getting into these sorts of messes, but he was realistic. He had always been more than a little accident-prone and it was not likely to change any time soon.

He replaced the green pouch and took off his backpack to call forth the healing potion. As it shimmered into view at the top of the pack, the gold coloured liquid in the small bottle appeared to swirl as if with a life of its own. He removed the glass stopper from the bottle and held it up to his lips to drink the entire bottle. He felt the strangely warm liquid run down the back of his throat and the magical glow filled his body as it did its work.

Gorrin felt invigorated and full of energy as all his cuts, scratches and bruises had mended and disappeared. He tapped the bottle on the ground three times and it was magically refilled with the gold, glittering liquid. The bottle was re-sealed with the stopper and then he carefully placed it back into his backpack, where it shimmered and disappeared from view.

He re-shouldered the backpack and looked around the forest. He could hear noises in the undergrowth and looked towards the sounds. He could just make out the shape of a couple of the New Forest ponies moving through the bracken and dead leaves. He smiled – it was good to be back in a forest again. He hadn't realised just how much he had missed it.

He continued along a rough path that threaded its way under the oak trees until it came out in a clearing. He took out his map and crystal and started to dowse again for his family. The crystal circled round and round, faster and faster, until he could feel the pull on the chain, as the stone pulled itself downwards towards the map, where there was a wooded area just south of a small hamlet called Ashurst marked on the map. It was only a few miles north of his location in the forest. It looked like that he had overshot his target only by a small margin.

As he continued to walk through the wooded area, the trees changed to a mixture of pine and oak, but eventually it was mainly pine. He became conscious, as he penetrated deeper into the coniferous forest that the light was dimming. The evergreen trees were so densely packed together, that they were screening out the light.

The dried pine needles crunched under his boots and the odour of pine reached him as he continued on under the dark canopy. Again, that odd sensation that he was being watched gradually stole over him. He had noticed that the sounds of the forest had suddenly vanished, as though it was holding its breath.

285

He was aware that this could be dangerous and so he decided to use the runic staff and the detection charm. As the delicate song etched itself into the air, the staff began to hum and vibrate. He swung the staff around until he could see that the runes on the staff were beginning to glow. Gorrin was ready to defend himself following his encounter with Horrin, should he need to, but he called out "Friend or foe, reveal yourself or I will fire my staff at you."

At first there was silence, then a voice that he had not heard for centuries, came to him from thin air, about four metres in front of him. "Gorrin, you want to be careful where you point that thing." As the voice came to him, a small figure dressed in woodland green shimmered into view. It was Morrin, his younger brother, although now his brother looked older than him.

Gorrin quelled the detection charm and lowered the staff and both brothers walked towards each other. They greeted in classic gnomic fashion, and then hugged each other as brothers. A gnomic greeting is like a handshake, but instead of gripping the other hand, you grasp the forearm.

Both started to speak at once, and then they both stopped. Gorrin fell silent to listen to his younger brother. "Where have you been? We all thought you were trapped, or worse. No one knew where you had gone, so we came looking for you. When we got to where your home was, there was no trace." The torrent of questions continued for a number of minutes, until

Morrin noticed that Gorrin was standing silent, but his face had taken on a scowl.

Gorrin understood, all too clearly what had happened. The protection charm on his home and the effects of the artefact that Horrin had booby-trapped his home with, had distorted the magic and greatly increased its effects. The protection spell had become so powerful, that even his own family had been unable to find him. This was something else that he 'owed' Horrin for.

Gorrin started to explain to Morrin, how he had become trapped and so had disappeared for more than three hundred and fifty years. At this news, it was Morrin's turn to scowl. Then he said: "Come Gorrin, you must see our new home in the forest. It really is very nice here now that the humans have made the forest a National Park, we should be safe here for many years to come."

The two then headed in the general direction of Ashurst, but kept to the pine forest until they came to a slight clearing in the trees where there was an embankment with a ditch running close by. Morrin sang a little song and a doorway shimmered into view, which he then opened, and they both headed inside. As the door closed behind them, the door shimmered again and vanished from view.

Inside, it was well lit by glowing blue stones and candles, and there was a wonderful aroma of cakes baking in an oven. Gorrin could see someone bending over the stove, and removing a baking tray on which there were spread blueberry muffins. As the figure stood up she turned around and froze as she caught sight of Gorrin standing in the doorway. The shock caused her to drop the tray of hot muffins on to the floor with a crash. The sound prompted Gorrin to rush forward and hug his mother with a vice like grip. There were tears in both their eyes as they hugged and kissed each other.

"Gorrin, my son, where have you been? I thought I would never see you again, but I always hoped that I might,." said Shorrin. Gorrin stepped back and held his mother at arms length so that he could look her full in the face. The years had been kind to her, but she was now quite old, even by gnomish standards.

The fact that Gorrin's face had apparently not aged was not lost on his mother either, as she carefully studied his lines and wrinkles – or rather the lack of them considering the centuries that had passed since they had last met.

At that moment, his father, Zorrin, made an appearance together with another brother Torrin. They were both investigating the crash and the noises of greetings in the kitchen. They both stopped in the doorway to stare at the newcomer, disbelieving what their eyes were telling them. They both rushed up to greet Gorrin with gnomic armshakes and hugs. Then they then started to fire question after question at him, not giving him chance to answer any of them.

When it became obvious that Gorrin had ceased trying to answer questions, they all grew quiet and looked anxiously at him and so he said, "Look, I am fine now. If we can sit down and have a nice cup of tea, I will tell you all about it."

And so with the mint tea and blueberry muffins that they had rescued from the floor, they went into the parlour and sat down at the table to eat warm muffins and drink tea. Gorrin had forgotten that they drank mint tea, as he had become used to drinking modern tea, but he politely kept silent on the matter.

Gorrin began to relate the story from the time when he had left them in 1649 until the present time and it was many hours later and several more cups of tea before he finished his story. When he reached the point in his story about his encounter with Horrin, there was a slight intake of breath, but Gorrin did not pick up on that.

It was not until he had finished telling his story that he noticed that his youngest sister Florrin and his elder brother Borrin were missing from the gathering. He had been so excited to see his family that he had completely missed that fact that they were still not here. "Where are the rest of the family?" he asked.

There was a silence as the other gnomes exchanged looks. Gorrin became concerned straight away, as he had seen the look on their faces. "Well, has something happened to them?"

His father spoke, "We don't know Gorrin. All we do know is that about one hundred and fifty years ago, Florrin left with her new husband to travel to Cornwall, where his family came from. We kept in touch by using the sunstones, but when we had to move from our home, the sunstones got broken or lost." The room had gone very quiet and all eyes looked at Gorrin.

"What happened to Borrin then?" queried Gorrin.

"Borrin went off into the world after that business with Horrin. He said he was heading north to see our Scottish cousins. But we haven't heard from him since either. We tried to contact him, by sunstone, but he never answered." Gorrin's eyebrows went up at this news, and then he continued, "Well what about Horrin?"

Everyone in the room shuddered at the mention of the name and frightened eyes darted around the room as they looked over their shoulders, as if to check to see he wasn't standing there.

Finally, Morrin spoke, "We don't talk about him any more Gorrin. Not since he escaped from the crystal. He has been seen around and about, but we try to keep clear of him. He has become much more powerful since that day when we first imprisoned him."

Gorrin's mother spoke up at this point. "Now enough of that, we are going to celebrate your return Gorrin. I am going to prepare a feast and we are all going to enjoy ourselves." She looked pointedly at Zorrin and got up to start to prepare the food. Gorrin stood up also, and offered to help, but she told him to sit down and have a chat with his father Zorrin. "Morrin and Torrin can give me a hand and you and father can talk."

It was several hours later, after they had all eaten a hearty meal and drank sloe gin as they were sitting around the blazing log fire that they started to talk again about the 'old days'. Outside, the weather had turned colder and there was sleet in the air. The winter was finally here and the snow would soon arrive.

He talked long into the night with his family, but one by one they grew sleepy and bid goodnight and went to bed. Gorrin was the last to leave and stared thoughtfully into the fire, as the flames flicked over the embers in the grate. He picked up the metal poker that nestled in its stand and poked the embers.

A shower of sparks shot up the chimney and he settled back in the armchair and continued to sip his drink. He put down the glass on the side table and continued to stare into the flickering flames. Gradually, his eyelids grew heavier and heavier. He was happy to have found his lost family, or at least most of it. His last thoughts before he went to sleep were "I wonder what happened to Borrin and Florrin?"

The End

~~~~~~~~~~~~~

Printed in the United Kingdom
by Lightning Source UK Ltd.
110641UKS00001B/11